SAVING GRACE

A. D. JUSTICE

Why Not?

lots of love

AD Justice

SAVING GRACE

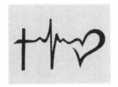

I wanted to ask for a divorce.

Instead of the fight I expected, she agreed—with a few stipulations, all of which revolved around our son leaving for college in the fall.

Keeping those promises would be a challenge, no doubt. But all I had to do was uphold my end of the deal then walk away without a backward glance.

Somewhere along the way, our charade became my reality.

With each day that passes, I realize time is once again my enemy. I can't lose her a second time. I'll never walk away—she healed my soul.

Saving Grace is now my only hope.

Cover designed by Okay Creations.

This book is dedicated to April.
You, my sweet friend, are an inspiration to everyone you meet.
Through the trials, your kindness never waivers. Despite the pain, your smile remains bright. Regardless of the setbacks, you look for the silver lining.
Thank you for answering all my questions, giving so much of yourself, and allowing me to use your Why Not idea.
I love you, sweet lady, and wish you nothing but love and happiness.
This world is a better place simply because you're in it.

CHAPTER 1

Grace

"I guess that's it, then." I fold the letter and slide it back into the envelope.

The weather outside fits my mood. Gray. Gloomy. Cold.

I move to the pantry and hide the letter somewhere no one else will find it—in the plastic canister under the bag of flour. With the airtight lid sealed, I push the container back into place while the tears stream down my face. Avoidance can only last for so long. I know, I've tried to use that tactic for dealing with problems far too long in my life. That method has never worked before, and I have too much to lose to use that approach again now.

The front door opens and slams shut a second later. "Mom, I'm home, and Wes's with me. We're going down the street to play video games at Alan's house. We'll be back later."

Heavy footsteps stomp up the stairs and back down again.

"Bye, Mom. Love you," Kyle calls out before he leaves.

"I love you too, baby," I reply. But he's already gone.

I remember my senior year of high school, and I desperately

want Kyle's to be different. Better. The best year of his life. He'll have enough problems to overcome in his life soon enough. While he's still with me, I'll do everything in my power to make his last year of childhood perfect.

As perfect as possible under the circumstances.

I have nine months before he leaves for college—from December until August. Nine months until all our lives change forevermore. My boy will be a man, and he will be focused on his own future. His own goals. His own path. His childhood will be over, and a new chapter will begin.

After I wipe the tears from my cheeks, I move back to my place at the door, staring out the solid sheet of glass at the snow-covered ground. Our Vermont winter started earlier than usual this year. The last few years, we've barely seen a dusting of snow in early December, but now the grass is already covered with at least an inch of the pure white precipitation.

"Grace?" Blake, my husband, walks in from the garage. He sounds tired after a long day at work.

"In the kitchen," I answer absently without turning around.

He walks into the room and lays his briefcase on the table. He releases a loud huff, and I visualize him running his fingers through his black hair. He's nervous and agitated, but he doesn't want to just blurt out what he has to say. I know Blake better than anyone—he would rather start a fight and tell me in a fit of anger than simply man up and come out with it.

"Did you work today?" His tone is already accusatory. He's preparing, setting up the fight he thinks is inevitable.

"No, I had some things to take care of, so I took the day off."

"And you couldn't cook dinner since you were already home?"

I turn to face him with a smile in place. "Of course I did. The food is holding warm in the oven. I'll make you a plate if you want to eat now."

His face falls, disappointment marring his normally handsome features. His attempt at starting a petty disagreement that would then escalate out of control didn't work. Under normal circumstances, I'd meet his ire with plenty of my own, and our shouting match would end in a silent standoff while we each wait for the other to give in first. As a nurse, I work just as hard, if not harder, than he does as a pharmaceutical representative. But that's not my response today—today, I'll react very differently for the sake of my son.

"I can do it myself after I change clothes," he mutters.

"Blake, have a seat. We need to talk," I say before he has a chance to leave the room.

The deer in the headlights expression on his face says it all. He's afraid of what I want to talk about. He doesn't get to be the one to lower the boom on me. I'm turning the tables and taking control of the situation. For the first time in the last several years, we're going to face our problems head on.

~

Blake

I REHEARSED my speech all the way home. My lines are solid, and my argument is sound. Grace has to see my reasoning and agree with me. The time has come and gone for us to be together any longer. Our marriage has become stagnant and cumbersome. The invisible millstone around my neck has weighed me down me for a long time. She has to feel the same way. The love we used to share is gone, and I don't see any way we can get it back. Too much time has passed, and we've allowed too much distance to come between us, even though we live in the same house.

The time to make a clean break is now. We both know it's true. We both feel it. The passion is gone, and we're more like roommates than lovers or a couple. After I pull into the driveway, I watch our son Kyle leave with his friend Wes. They're headed down the street to another friend's house, no doubt to play video games for hours or enjoy a little street hockey. Now is my chance to put an end to the charade we've been living in, moving through each day like detached zombies. Grace and I will be alone and can use the privacy to work out the details of an agreement.

I'm going to tell her I want a divorce.

When I walk in and see her standing at the sliding glass door at the back of the house, her long brown hair cascading over her shoulders and down her back, my plans to spring my request on her fly right out the window. A knife stabs my heart, twisting inside until it nearly steals my breath. The reasons that stop me today are the same ones that have stopped me every day for the last six months. She hasn't done one thing wrong to justify my actions.

She's the same woman I fell in love with eighteen years ago when I was only nineteen. But then again, she's not the same at all. We've both changed, and time has separated us instead of brought us closer. But I don't want to hurt her. I don't want to be the reason she cries. Guilt eats me alive because I know I have to tell her now—it's literally now or never.

It's not just guilt, though. It's knowing, deep down, I'll never stop loving her, and I'll never truly have the connection we once had again with another living soul. But I don't feel wanted or needed here—by her or by my son. The useless third wheel I've become has driven me to the point where I think it would be best if I just disappeared from their lives altogether. The words are on the tip of my tongue, and the bitterness makes it impossible to swallow.

Then she shocks me with her demand. "Blake, have a seat. We need to talk."

Nothing good ever comes from those words. They're always followed by bad news. I know, because I planned to use the same phrase to get her attention and set the tone for our conversation.

My mind churns as I slide into the chair, and she sits across the table from me. Maybe she's about to ask me for a divorce, knowing we fell out of step with each other long ago. Maybe it's another mundane detail about the house I've forgotten to handle. Maybe an overdue bill I neglected to pay. This is what my life has been reduced to, and whether it hurts her or not, I don't think I can take it one more day without imploding.

"I know about Tammy."

Her voice is so calm and collected, I question for a second if I imagined her words.

"And I know you've been planning to ask me for a divorce for some time now so you can be free to run away with her. You think if you leave all your responsibilities behind, you can be the carefree teenager you were before we married."

I've never been stunned speechless. But I have no words—nothing will come out of my slack-jawed mouth. My lips refuse to move in my defense. My mind screams at me to lie—to hold on to my last shred of pride and decency as a man...a husband...a father. But my tongue refuses to cooperate.

"We married so young. The adjustment was hard on both of us. Then six months later, we had Kyle, and he took all our attention and time. Raising him took precedence over everything in our lives. Surviving day after day took all our energy. Now that we've reached the point where he's no longer dependent on us, we've forgotten how to be a couple.

"Then you found someone else, and our relationship never had a chance. So you think Tammy makes you happy, and she makes you feel like a man again. You have a chance at a new life with her, to regain your vitality and feel alive again."

She pierces me with her assessing gaze, making me feel like an insect under a microscope. She knows me too well—she always has. Listening to her use many of the very words I'd planned to say makes me realize how clichéd they all sound.

"Grace," I start, finally finding my voice.

"Don't." Her voice is firm and resolute. Whatever else she has to say, she has already made up her mind to follow through. That's one thing I can say about my wife. Once her mind is set, there's no changing it.

"Don't tell me that you're sorry. That it just has to be this way. That we both know it's best. You listen to me, Blake Hardy, and you listen well. A divorce is not what's best right now. This is Kyle's senior year of high school, and he deserves the best we can give him. Your running off with your little whore is nowhere in the same realm as what's best for him.

"I've given this a lot of thought. If you disagree, and insist on fucking up what should be the best year your son has in school, know that I'll use every conceivable means to destroy you. You'll be left with nothing. But if you agree and abide by all the rules, you can have your divorce, along with everything we have."

"Everything?" I can't even form an intelligent response. She has thoroughly stunned me.

"The house, the furniture, savings, retirement accounts—whatever you want. This is for Kyle, not for me. He leaves for college in nine months. Surely you can survive being married to me for that much longer."

My curiosity is piqued. Why would she even suggest this after finding out about Tammy? What is she up to?

"What are your terms?"

~

Grace

EARLIER THIS MORNING, my best friend came over to be my sounding board. Leigh Brydon has been in my life for as long as I can remember. We started in elementary school together and finished nursing school together. If anyone will be in my corner, it's her. My mind was made up as far as my plan, but I needed her support more than anything. She thought of things I didn't, but I knew I'd never be able to pull this off without her help, without her support, without her guidance.

"Blake is cheating on me," I blurted out.

She stopped moving, her hand halfway to her mouth with the cup of coffee I'd just poured. "You're sure?"

"Without a doubt. I hired a private investigator to follow him and get the details on the other woman." I pushed hair behind my ear and stared at my coffee cup.

"That son of a bitch!" She slammed her mug down on the table, ignoring the hot java that splashed on her hand. "You need help castrating him? I have gardening shears. Then we can go after her. Bet he'll think twice about her after we fucking scalp her."

God, I loved my best friend more in that moment that the rest of the previous decades I've known her.

"Let me guess," she continued her rant. "She's in her twenties. No kids. Flat stomach. Perky breasts. And no real-life experiences to jade her."

"Wow, Leigh, sounds like you've met Tammy George before."

"So the whore's name is Tammy George, huh? We can find her house and take the bitch down."

I laughed—and I needed that laugh more than Leigh knew. "No need. I know where she lives, where she works, and what she drives. I probably know more about her now than Blake does."

"How long have you known about this?" She was suddenly serious, and she'd finally realized I wasn't freaking out like she was.

"For about two months now. He's been seeing her for about six months, though."

"And you haven't killed him yet? Or even confronted him? Or slashed her tires?" Leigh's shocked face was almost comical. Except, the only reason she wore that expression was because my life was falling to pieces. "I would've already killed Alex in his sleep if it were me."

"When I first found out, I planned on ambushing them on one

of their dates. Making a scene. Destroying their careers—since they work together. Then destroying their cars. But I stopped myself for Kyle's sake. I have to consider how this will hurt my son."

"I know that look, Grace. You've come up with some crazy plan I'm not going to like at all, haven't you?"

"Yes. You'll hate it. But I need you, Leigh. I need you in my corner, reminding me that everything I do is for my son. You know how strained my relationship with my parents is. They've never forgiven me for getting pregnant in high school and marrying Blake. I don't want to give them more ammunition to make our lives hell. This is the hardest thing I've ever done, but I have to see it through."

Leigh took a long sip of her coffee then met my gaze directly. "All right. Let's hear this brilliant plan of yours. You know I'm always in your corner, and I will do whatever you need me to do to get you through this. Don't think for one second that I'm doing it for that motherfucker you're married to, though."

"I'm not doing it for him either. This is for Kyle." Then I shared my plan, step by step.

～

I swallow down the bile rising in my throat, run my fingers through my thick hair, and prepare myself to present my solution to Blake. I'm finding it hard to look at him without ripping him to shreds. I want to scream and cry and freak the fuck out on him before I tell him to get out and never come back. I want to light all of his clothes on fire and laugh maniacally while I watch them burn to ashes. Then my eyes float to the senior portrait of Kyle we had made just before Blake's sordid affair started, and my focus is immediately back on my son.

"Number one, you're going to be the father you used to be to Kyle. You will spend time with him having fun. No bitching, no complaining, no paying more attention to your phone than to your son. Take him to concerts. Go camping. Go snowboarding with him. I don't care what you two do—whatever he wants to do —but don't let him feel like he's second to anything or anyone outside of this house."

Blake narrows his eyes slightly, draws his brows down, and tilts his head. I can see the gears turning in his mind as he tries to work out the next step my plan because the first stipulation is too easy.

"Okay. Spend time focused on Kyle. Got it. What's number two?"

"Number two, you're going to be the husband you used to be whenever Kyle is around. You'll show interest in me, my day, what I want. You'll sit next to me when we watch TV. You'll eat dinner at the table with us. You'll show Kyle every day what a real, loving husband looks like. He looks up to you. I will not let you ruin his chances for a happy marriage by setting an example of a shitty husband now."

"So we'll pretend we're still madly in love when Kyle's here." His question is more of a statement, and the pain it causes knocks the breath out of me.

"Yes. We'll both have to pretend we can stand the sight and touch of each other," I retort. My arrow hits the bull's-eye. He winces, visibly wounded from my remark. "Kyle and his girlfriend were here the other evening…when you weren't…and I noticed him treating her with the same disregard you show me. They had a fight about it, and I talked to him after he took her home. You're already rubbing off on him."

Blake takes a few seconds to consider my words, the weight of the world on his shoulders showing in the lines on his face. He closes his eyes briefly, inhales deeply, then releases it with a resigned huff. "I guess if you can do it, I can do it. And number three?"

CHAPTER 2

Blake

So far, Grace has completely floored me with her requests. When she first mentioned Tammy, I expected the worst knock-down, drag-out fight we've ever had. I expected tears and screaming—and threats. I honestly expected her to make every threat under the sun: to keep me, to get rid of me, to hurt me. I've entertained all sorts of scenarios—from her begging me to stay to her saying she also had someone else. But she surprised me—with a list of compromises and expectations centered around Kyle and our family instead. I can't disagree with anything she has said; I'm just surprised as shit she's saying it.

And that hurts like hell because it means she doesn't love me anymore. She doesn't care *if* I leave—only *when* I leave. There's a part of me deep inside that still loves her, even if I haven't felt *in love* with her for so long now. But somehow, hearing her say she can't stand being around me slices me to the core.

Now, I'm waiting for number three. Waiting for the other shoe to fall. I'm getting off way too easy so far. I can't say I'd be so generous with the compassion and understanding if I were in her shoes, which throws up another giant red flag for me. Promises of not fighting me for anything in the divorce if I abide by all her rules can't be all there is to this. She must have some hidden agenda, but she's ten steps ahead of me, and my mind is reeling as I try to catch up. There must be a catch somewhere in this agreement, something that will test me to my limits of sanity.

"Number three is you will stop seeing Tammy until the day after Kyle leaves for college. Once he's settled in, you can do whatever you want with your twenty-three-year-old slut. If you slip up and make one phone call or send one text, all bets are off, and you leave here with nothing but the clothes on your back."

"You want me to stop seeing her for *nine months?*"

"Blake, if what the two of you have is really love, it'll still be true love in nine months. You can live without her for that long. You will not disrespect me by continuing to fuck someone else while you sleep under my roof. These conditions are not negotiable. Take them or leave them. And God help you if you leave them."

I run my hand through my hair in frustration. Nine months without seeing, hearing, or touching Tammy? How am I supposed to do that when I'm in love with her? When I can't wait to see her every day? When I rush to work just because I know she's there?

"What about my job? I can't just up and quit. How do you think I can go to work and not see her?"

The pain in Grace's eyes shreds me. She deserves so much better than me—than what I can give her. Than what I have given her. We both had such big plans for the future when we were Kyle's age. Well, when Grace was his age anyway.

She was only seventeen when we got pregnant and barely eighteen when we married. I was nineteen and had graduated a year before she did. She went through most of her senior year pregnant, enduring the stares, pointing fingers, and whispers behind her back without me by her side. I'd already started college and was almost halfway through my sophomore year when I had to drop out to support my new bride and soon-to-be-born baby.

I was angry about that for a long time, though I never let anyone know. Angry with myself for not being more careful. Angry at the world for changing my plans. Just angry about everything and nothing. My lack of education and inability to get anything more than a shitty, low-paying job created more than a financial hardship for us in the early years. Had it not been for my parents, we might have been homeless and starving. Grace's parents were furious with her for electing to keep our baby, but they were beyond livid when she announced she was marrying me. They disowned her for more than a decade. They've only reestablished a connection in the last several years, and it's still not a solid one.

Memories flood my mind, and the past comes rushing at me with a new ferocity. The memories of how we used to be together are what make me second-guess my decision to leave Grace. We used to have so much love. I've pushed those memories and feelings aside so many times over the last few years, but especially over the last six months. Losing our love and the closeness we once had felt like a literal death of a loved one, and when I'd dealt with the disappointment for so long, I couldn't take it anymore. That's when I found Tammy. That's when I found my vigor for life and love again.

"Are you afraid she won't love you in nine months? Afraid absence doesn't make the heart grow fonder? Afraid your side of the bed won't have a chance to get cold?" Grace fires her questions at me, and I know I deserve it, but they each hit a sensitive chord in me. I've questioned my own worth so often, I shouldn't be upset when Grace verbalizes my insecurities. But I can't stop my knee-jerk reaction. It stings.

"You haven't answered my question. Do you expect me to quit my job to avoid seeing her?"

"I expect you to go out of your way to avoid seeing her, taking her phone calls, reading her texts, or anything else to do with her. But quitting your job won't be necessary. I had a long talk with your boss. There's a no-fraternization rule in the office, you know. Both of you could be—and should be—fired for your actions. But Rob has agreed to let you work from home instead of going into the office. You can still visit your doctors, but if you go back into the office without his permission, you'll both be fired."

"You have thought this through. I have to admit, I didn't know you cared so much about me anymore. I mean, you've been busy gathering information about me and talking to my boss behind my back. Making plans for my job and where I'll work. I guess to everyone else, you just look like the loving wife who's loyal and only trying to do what's right. They probably don't know you're holding it over my head to control me and get what you want."

"Rob was going to fire you tomorrow for your blatant disregard of the company rules and, apparently, company time. I saved your job by talking to him when I did, getting him to give us a chance to get back on our feet. I had no idea your head was on the chopping block until I talked to him today. I bet you had no clue either. Thinking with your dick instead of your head will do that to you," she fires back.

Touché. She's got me there. Again. I'm surprised the daggers shooting from her eyes haven't penetrated my jugular yet.

"What's your decision, Blake? Be a man. Make up your mind and stick with whatever choice you make. There's no going back either way."

"Not that I have much choice since I need my job, but you're right. Kyle deserves to have the best senior year we can give him. My word doesn't mean much now, I know. But I promise I will stick to your rules until the day after Kyle leaves for college. Then you and I will go our separate ways."

"You'll understand if I insist you tell her right now, in front of me. And show her you mean business. If you cave to her whining, even a little, you can walk out the door and never come back here again."

I hesitate for a second, only because I think this conversation is better held in private, but Grace insists. So I put my phone on speaker and call Tammy. The line rings, and I cringe, not knowing what she'll say when she answers or how she'll react to the news with no more of an explanation than I can give her.

"Why aren't you here with me? I'm in bed and had to get started without you. But if you're real bad, I'll let you catch up." The buzzing in the background confirms she has her vibrator on high. The anger and hurt in Grace's eyes bore through me. The thrill of sneaking around just lost much of its luster.

"Tammy, you're on speaker. I'm sitting here with Grace. She knows everything."

The buzzing stops.

"Oh. Shit."

"Yeah. So, listen. Grace and I have just had a long talk, and a few things are going to change for the next nine months. This coming year is a monumental one for our son—he's graduating high school and starting college. We're focusing on his well-being and what's best for him in the long run.

"Grace and I talked about a divorce and how that would affect Kyle right when he needs to stay focused on school. I agree with Grace's ultimatum, Tammy. You and I can't see each other until he starts college. It's only nine months away. I know that sounds like a long time, but believe me, it'll fly by before you know it, and we can be together again."

Grace wipes a tear off her cheek, and I realize how insensitive I'm being to her. The time will fly by, but there's no reason for me to rub that in her face.

Then Tammy replies.

"Nine months? You expect me to wait for you for nine long months while you stay there and play house with your *wife*? You said you weren't fucking her anymore. You said you wanted to be with *me*. What do you really want, Blake? Do you want her, or do you want me?"

"It's not that simple, Tammy. Grace and I have a son to think about and provide for—and we have to consider how our decisions will impact his future. I can't just up and leave him when he needs me the most. I'm not asking that much of you. If I were in the military, I'd be deployed for longer than that. I've made my decision, and I'm standing by it—for Kyle. You and I can be together again in September. Until then, I've agreed not to talk to you or see you in any way. I'm asking you to remember you also said you love me. Now prove it and wait for me."

"Blake, I do love you. But I don't know what'll happen in that much time—nine months is a *long time*. How can I say where I'll be or what I'll be doing by then? I mean, I know I'll miss you like crazy. I'll try, Blake—I'll try to wait for you and live without you until then. I can't make any promises, though. I just don't understand any of this."

Grace rolls her eyes then shoots me a dirty look when she leans toward the phone to speak. "It's very simple, Tammy. Do not call, text, or try to contact my husband in any way. One call from me to Rob, and you can kiss your job goodbye. When Blake is available to catch up with your masturbation schedule, he'll let you know."

"Uh. Okay."

That bright light shining into the dark corners of my secrets is harsh and reveals things I haven't noticed before—and didn't want to see now. Like how inexperienced and inarticulate Tammy really is when it comes to dealing with conflict. I try to push those thoughts aside since I blindsided her with a joint phone call with my wife. Had the situation been reversed, I'm not sure how I'd react if I were in her shoes. If she can give me the next nine months, I can give her the benefit of the doubt.

But not seeing, hearing, or touching Tammy for that long will be pure hell. Keeping these promises to Grace will test my self-control to no end. Just when I started to feel alive again, the carpet gets yanked out from under my feet.

~

Grace

I QUESTION my sanity for the hundredth time since Blake and I sat down for this talk. But it's done—his job, his livelihood, the name he's worked so hard to build in the medical community—it's all on the line, and he won't risk his reputation more than he already has. People talk; that's one truth I can always count on. If he screws this up, a lot of people will do a lot of talking. That's the last thing he'd want to happen.

We spent last night the same as we've done most every other night for the past six months. I went upstairs to bed, and Blake fell asleep on the couch in the living room downstairs. That used to bother me because I could feel us growing apart. But last night, I couldn't have slept in the same bed with him if someone had held a gun to my head. Just the thought of him anywhere near me made me sick to my stomach. Though I've known about Tammy for a while, hearing her voice and the things she said to my husband were too much to take.

I move through the motions as I get ready for work while it's still pitch-black outside. December is colder than usual, and I'll feel it when I walk into the hospital before daylight. These twelve-hour shifts are long, but I love the time off it allows me. Three days on, four days off. Those three days working in ICU are hell, but the four-day-long furlough every week more than makes up for it.

When I walk downstairs, I'm surprised to find Blake already awake and dressed. He never starts work as early as I do.

"I, uh, thought we could go by my office to pick up a few things then I'll drop you off at the hospital. No one will be there this early in the morning, and I'll apparently be around to pick you up tonight since I'm working from home now."

He looks uncomfortable. Unsure. But at least he's making a halfway attempt to uphold our agreement. Even if I do feel more like a prison warden watching his every move and keeping him locked up in a comfortable cell than his wife that he willingly married more than eighteen years ago.

"Okay," I reply, equally uncomfortable.

We're quiet while walking out to his car. It's still dark out, but I can see my breath in the air. "Feels like we're going to have a bad winter," I say as I slide into the passenger seat. When in doubt, talk about the weather.

"Yeah, that's what they're predicting. Tammy said..." His voice fades away, aware of the blunder he just made. Aware that the coldness in the car now has nothing to do with the temperature outside.

"I know you don't believe me, but I meant Tammy Young—our neighbor down the street. I realized how it must have sounded to you the second it left my mouth."

"It's fine." My voice is impassive, but inside, I'm furious. I'll never be able to hear that name again without associating it with the worst time in my life. "What did Tammy Young say?"

"She swears by the *Farmers' Almanac*. According to their prediction, we'll have a completely white Christmas this year. It'll be the first one we've had in a decade."

"I remember. Kyle was only seven, and we took him out to look at all the Christmas lights in the snow. He watched the sky for Santa and Rudolph instead." The memory of that time in our lives hurts, and tears sting the back of my eyes. Our relationship was so different then. "We had a snowball fight after Kyle opened his presents. We let him win."

Blake chuckles. "I'd forgotten all about that."

Yeah, you've forgotten a lot of important things lately, is on the tip of my tongue, but I damn near bite it off to keep from saying the words aloud.

"How could I have forgotten that?"

He isn't really asking me. His face is pained, and his voice is strained. He covers his mouth with his hand, deep in thought as he drives. He's silent for the rest of the way to his office. When we park in front of the mostly dark office building, he turns to me.

"Do you want to come in?"

"No. I'll wait out here."

"Okay. I won't be long."

CHAPTER 3

Blake

*W*alking to the door of my office building, I realize nothing about this situation has gone the way I thought it would. Deep down, I'd pictured the whole conversation and what would occur between us. I'd felt the despair I'd cause her after I revealed my secrets, and knowing how much it would hurt her has been what's prevented me from going through with it. Every day, I'd assure Tammy I would tell Grace that night. Every night when I got home, I'd see Grace and stop short when I pictured how she'd respond.

I thought Grace would scream and cry, then beg me not to go.

I thought I'd tell her we were over and I was moving on with Tammy.

I thought Tammy and I would move in together.

I thought I'd finally be happy again.

Instead, I'm going up to my office to clear it out, to take home the things I need to do my job.

I'm leaving the woman I love behind for the next nine months.

I'm not even sure she'll still want me then. She said she loves me, but even that's in question now.

My wife didn't scream, cry, or threaten me once. Not really. She already knew about Tammy and me. She already knew I'd ask for a divorce. Then she beat me to the punch and offered to give me everything I want in the divorce if I just wait until our son is out of the house. At this point, I don't think she even cares about me or what I do. As long as Kyle is taken care of, my needs don't matter.

I pass Tammy's desk on my way to my office and stop for a moment. I'm so tempted to leave her a note—to remind her to wait for me, to say I love her, to tell her I miss her. But I force myself to keep walking instead. With my luck, someone else would find it first and send it to Grace. Then I'd be royally screwed.

With my laptop and files packed in my briefcase, I close the door to my office behind me, fully aware of how the physical action feeds the metaphorical one in my mind. The door is shut, there's no going back, and my future is more uncertain than at any other time in my life. I feel as if I'm stepping into a hopeless vacuum—no love, no joy, and nothing to look forward to in the near future.

There's no point in even glancing at Tammy's desk when I leave. If she and I survive this separation, we'll be stronger for it. If not, we were never meant to be anyway. The only certainty I have at the moment is Grace and I will be divorced come summer's end. There's no saving our marriage at this point. That fact is abundantly clear.

But her memory of that white Christmas so many years ago hit me especially hard. The finality of it all. How fleeting time is and how things change right before our eyes without us even real-izing it. We were happy once as a family. We were happy once as a couple. Then, all of a sudden, we weren't happy anymore.

With a heavy sigh, I yank the back door of my car open and

drop my overstuffed briefcase inside before I take my place behind the wheel. Grace doesn't even acknowledge me. That shouldn't surprise me—we stopped paying attention to each other years ago. I glance at the clock as I put the car into drive.

"You're going into work a little early today, aren't you?"

"Yeah, I have a few things to take care of before my shift starts."

"All right." She's being as vague as she can, shutting me out of her day. "I'll be there to pick you up when you get off work tonight."

When I stop in front of the hospital, she reaches for the door handle then stops. She takes a second to collect her thoughts before turning to look at me. "Thank you for trying. I do appreciate that you agreed to put in the effort. But if you decide to go back on your word, tell me first. You at least owe me that much respect."

All I can do is nod in agreement. Her straightforward, no emotion involved request is so unlike the woman I fell in love with, I'm not sure I know this woman in front of me now. Nostalgia hits me square in the chest, and I wish like mad I could go back in time to when we were still a "we" and change anything that drove us in separate directions. But wishful thinking has never gotten me anywhere, and I can't keep up the separate lives we've created.

After I set up my workstation in our home office and handled my early morning emails, I made my rounds to the doctors' offices in my assigned specialty. Two of my physicians' groups took up most of my day, but I had a difficult time keeping my train of thought on the correct rails. Alternating between Tammy, Kyle, and Grace left me mentally drained.

Driving through our neighborhood, memories of Kyle and me doing a variety of things together overwhelm my senses. Going house to house trick or treating at Halloween, admiring all the neighbors' Christmas lights, enjoying the warmth of a bright spring day, walking him to his friend's house in the heat of the summer—we've had so many good times right here. When I walk into our house, I find Kyle is already home from school.

"Hey, Dad. What are you doing home so early?"

"I moved my office here. I'll be working from home for a while."

"Cool. You should've done that years ago. Mom and I used to talk about how many hours you put in every week."

"Oh, yeah? What did you two have to say about that?"

"Just how we never got to see you because you were always in the office, in meetings, or away at conferences. I bet Mom is glad to have you home with her on her days off now."

"Yeah, I'm sure she will be," I lie. But his words strike an unintended target in me. Was I really always gone from their lives? "Listen, Kyle, I've been thinking. Your mom brought up something we did when you were little. I think it'd be fun to do it again now."

"What is it?"

I remind him of the night we walked the neighborhood to look at the lights, and his eyes brighten when he recalls the details.

"Yeah, that'd be pretty cool. We should do that one night. Maybe Tracy can come with us. Then I can show off our neighborhood to my girlfriend." He pulls a bag of chips from the pantry and settles down in front of the TV.

An idea begins to form when I follow him into the den. The more I think about it, the more it takes root in my mind. And the more I want to see it through. "I have an even better idea. Let's go cut a Christmas tree and put it up before your mom gets off work. We can surprise her."

Kyle cuts his eyes over at me and stares for several seconds, his face contorted as if I've grown an additional head. "Okay, what gives? What's really going on here?"

Grace hasn't told him anything about our arrangement, I know this for sure. But ice still flows through my veins, heading straight for my heart, as fear grips me. How *had* I planned to tell Kyle about Tammy?

"What do you mean?"

"Come on, Dad. You're working at home all of a sudden, and now you're making all these plans to do family holiday stuff. You've never done that before. Who's dying?"

"It's nothing like that, Kyle." I laugh and shake my head. "Your mom said something to me that really hit home. You're leaving in nine months and going off to college. You'll be a different man when you come home. We need to make the most of the time we have while you're still here."

He eyes me suspiciously before replying. "All right, but we're not going to become one of those weird families that spends all their time together. I still have plans with my friends."

"I think we can squeeze your friends in once or twice before your graduation."

"All right, all right." He laughs and drops the bag of chips on the couch beside him. I see so much of the little boy I raised in the man who's in front of me now. "So, a Christmas tree, huh? We haven't put one up since I started high school."

"Yeah, well, it's about time to rectify that, don't you think?"

He turns off the TV and grabs his coat from the back of the couch. "Let's go chop down a tree for Mom. But if she gets pissed because she has to decorate it, you're helping her. Not me."

"Fair enough," I chuckle. 'Let's go. We have to get this done before she gets off work since I'm picking her up."

"Yeah, why'd you take her to work? You never carpool."

I shrug, hiding my guilt. "I had to leave early anyway, so I just dropped her off on my way back. Let's go. You're wasting time."

A couple of hours later, Kyle and I are home with the biggest damn tree they had, along with bags upon bags of brand-new lights, bows, and other decorations. Neither of us knew if Grace had saved any of our old ones, so we stopped by the store and filled the shopping cart full of bright and shiny Christmas cheer.

The scent from the fresh-cut tree and authentic garland soon fills the house, putting both Kyle and me in the spirit even more. We work together to put up the icicle lights along the eaves of the house and set the lighted reindeer in the yard.

"Mom's going to love this, Dad." Kyle stands back and admires our work. "This should earn us a few brownie points. I can't wait to see her face. I'll plug it all in when you pull into the driveway. She'll be so surprised."

"Good plan, son. Give it about an hour before you come out here and wait for us, though. I still have to pick her up and get back home." I ruffle his hair the way I used to when he was still shorter than me. Before he grew up. Before I blinked and too much time had already passed.

~

Grace

"HOW WAS WORK?" Blake asks after I shut the car door.

"Fine. How as your day?" I'm really trying to be civil, but this is harder than I thought it would be.

"Good. I met with a couple of my large physician groups and had great discussions about a breakthrough drug we're bringing to market. Then Kyle and I hung out for a few hours. We actually had a great time—just talking and doing guy stuff."

"I'm glad to hear that. He needs his father around."

"You're right, he does. But he needs you too."

"He has me." My tone is matter-of-fact. *I'm not the one who planned to leave him.* "Blake, I think you need to go get checked for STDs. You may trust her, but you just never know what someone you trusted is capable of hiding from you."

"I appreciate your concern," he replies, his sarcasm barely detectable. "But..." He hesitates. "There was never a time I wasn't protected. I wouldn't chance that or any other kind of surprise."

24

No, you wouldn't chance that, but you would gamble with your own family.

I think it, but I don't say it. One step at a time. One day at a time.

"Grace, I know what you're thinking."

"Really? You think so? What am I thinking?"

"I didn't mean to fall in love with someone else. It just happened. That doesn't make her a bad person."

"What does make her a bad person, then, Blake? The fact that she was sneaking around, sleeping with a married man obviously doesn't. So I guess she's just the epitome of the perfect woman. She's your soul mate, huh?"

"Maybe she is. She certainly acts more like it than you do. She looks at me like I'm the sexiest man alive. She wants to be with me, to talk to me, to touch me. You haven't even looked at me in I don't know how long, much less wanted me. You've been in your own little world, focused only on Kyle. That's fine—you should've been active in his life, but not his exclusively. Not to the point I'm shut out of your life."

"Well, I guess you were just the perfect husband for the last eighteen years, and I've always been your shitty wife. Duly noted. But for the record, you don't even know me. You've never tried to get to know me since Kyle was born. You've withdrawn from both of us more and more every year. You've blamed us for why you had to put your dream of going to medical school behind you.

"You've blamed us for why you had to settle for a bachelor's degree from night school and a pharmaceutical representative position that allows you to work with doctors but never be one of them. That wasn't my fault, and it wasn't Kyle's fault. Last I checked, it took both of us to conceive him. And, to prove my point, that wasn't what I was thinking at all. I was thinking about how you didn't mind taking a chance with your family's lives, so why wouldn't you chance anything else?"

We're silent for the rest of the ride, but the tension in the car is as thick as molasses. Over the last several minutes, I've mentally kicked my own ass for spewing all the vitriol like I did. I'd resolved to make this arrangement as painless and platonic as possible. I accepted the fate of my marriage months ago when I first confirmed his affair, but I want Kyle's last days at home to be pleasant memories...something I didn't have at his age.

"Grace, I'm sorry. I shouldn't have said all that to you. It was insensitive and uncalled for. We're both doing the best we can under the circumstances, and I don't want to make it any harder on either of us. Can we start the evening over?"

"I'd like that. I apologize for the things I said and the way I said them, too."

"Apology accepted, but not needed. I hate to admit it, but maybe there's some truth to what you said. And if it makes you feel better, I'll get tested and give you the results. You don't trust me and I don't blame you, but I'm telling you the truth."

"I'd feel better if you did. No one needs any surprises in the future."

"Consider it done, then."

Tears threaten to fall when we turn onto our street. Nothing about this predicament is how my life was supposed to go. Then he slows as we approach our driveway, and the entire front of the house illuminates with beautiful white twinkling lights. Icicles hang down across the front porch. A family of brightly lit deer is standing on the front lawn. The shrubs are covered with multicolored lights, and small, festive trees complete the scene.

"What? When did you—? How?" I can't even form a complete question or gather my thoughts.

"Kyle and I decided to surprise you. We haven't decorated or been out to see the neighborhood lights together in a long time. So, we grabbed a few things at the store and set this up."

"It's beautiful. You two did a great job." Suddenly, my door is jerked open, and Kyle stands there with a huge, toothy grin on his face.

"Mom, you gotta come watch this. The deer's head moves up and down like he's eating." Kyle grabs my hand and pulls me out of the car and across the snow-covered grass. "Watch him!"

I can barely tear my eyes from Kyle to look at the decorative animals. The wonder of Christmas is there in his eyes, twinkling with the lights he helped put up all over the house. "I love it, Kyle. You and your dad outdid yourselves."

"Well, we may have another surprise for you inside. Come see!"

With that, we're off like a shot toward the front door. Blake chuckles as he comes up behind us. "Kyle, slow down. Your mom has been on her feet all day. I'm sure she's tired."

Kyle stops and looks at me, absorbing his dad's words. Then he shrugs and picks me up, cradling me to his chest, and resumes his sprint. I can't help but laugh at his antics, but his thoughtfulness warms my heart and gives me hope.

"Kyle, put me down, you lunatic. I can walk the rest of the way."

"Nope. We're already there now." He sets me down on the porch, and I turn in a full circle, admiring all their work.

"This looks beautiful. I love it."

"Wait until you see inside." Kyle smiles and opens the front door.

The aroma of fresh balsam pine surrounds me, and I take a deep breath to draw it in. Then I see the garland and decorations inside the house, and I can barely move from shock. My feet feel heavy, rooted to the wooden slats beneath them, but Kyle takes my hand and pulls me inside.

Our home is a two-story Victorian with more room than the three of us need, but Blake and I were so thrilled when we were finally able to buy it. The foyer is covered in wreaths, and garland is wrapped around the banister leading upstairs. Tiny white lights alternate between burning brightly and fading to black, making our home intimate and inviting.

Then my eyes land on the enormous tree standing tall close to the fireplace. "This is amazing. You two definitely surprised me with all this. Did you leave the tree for me to decorate?"

"Yep. We didn't know what decorations you'd kept from years ago or which ones you'd want to use," Blake explains. "We bought a bunch of new ornaments and bows today, if you want to use those too." He can't hide his excitement over his handiwork.

I gush over their hard work and thoughtfulness with sincerity. I'm very touched at the lengths they went to simply to surprise me.

Huh. My husband seems a little embarrassed by my praise.

I pull my hair up in a quick ponytail and work through my fatigue to fully decorate the tree with the new ornaments. Kyle helps, though he tries to hide that he really wants to. Blake watches as Kyle and I laugh and joke with each other. He has an odd expression on his face, and he's quieter than usual. But he's with us, and he's trying. I have to give him credit for that, at least.

"There's one box from the attic I need to get," I say when I stand back and admire the tree. "It has the ornaments Kyle made in elementary school in it."

After I climb the stairs, I stop to catch my breath before pulling the steps to the attic down from the ceiling. When I put my foot on the first step, Blake's voice startles me.

"Let me get it for you, Grace." He's standing close, and his voice is low and intimate. Or my mind is playing tricks on me. "You must be tired after working more than twelve hours today. Plus, that box may be heavy."

Just a few days ago, I would've argued and said I could do it myself. Tonight, I recognize he just wants to be helpful. He's showing Kyle ways to be a good husband. He's keeping up his end of the deal. So I let him.

"Okay, Blake. I'll go up and find it, then you can bring it down-stairs. Thank you."

"I'll come up with you. We may have to move stuff around to get to the right box."

I turn to climb up to the attic and feel Blake close on my heels. When I reach the top step, he puts his hands on my hips to help push me up the last big step. The contact is too much. The genuine way he wants to help throws me off-kilter. Memories of how we used to be together hurt too much to think about. Inside the cramped quarters of the attic, Blake and I are way too close.

This wasn't part of the deal.

CHAPTER 4

Blake

Grace checks the boxes, and I move them out of her way when she doesn't find what she's looking for. We're working as a team again for the first time in what feels like forever. If only we'd started this a few years ago—working together to meet a goal—maybe we could've salvaged our marriage.

But I can't live in a loveless marriage anymore. She cringed when I touched her. I was only helping her up the final step, but I felt her tense under my hand the second I made contact with her. She can't even stand the thought of me in her presence anymore, and I can't really blame her now. But this vicious cycle is what pushed us to this point in the first place.

She opens another box and freezes in place. Her face falls, and tears glisten in her eyes. I have a sinking feeling in the pit of my stomach.

"What is it, Grace?"

She lifts an ornament from years ago. It's a homemade picture frame, and the photo is of all three of us. Grace and I are Mrs.

Claus and Santa Claus, and Kyle is an elf. We'd volunteered at the homeless shelter that year, spending our family time with less fortunate people. Kyle said it was the best Christmas we'd ever given him, because we were more grateful for what we already had instead of wishing we had more.

I never would've guessed a twelve-year-old boy's words would prove to be wiser than anything I'd said in my thirty-eight years— all the way up until today.

"That was a great Christmas, wasn't it?" I prompt her, trying to get her to respond.

"It was the best. You told me you wanted to try for a baby that night."

Fuck. I'd forgotten that part, but of course she remembered it.

"It wasn't meant to be, Grace."

"Yeah, well, I guess you'll have that with Tammy now." She picks up the box and starts toward the step.

I put my hand on her arm to stop her. "Why do you say that?"

She throws a disgusted huff over her shoulder. "Blake, seriously? She's young—only in her early twenties. Of course she'll expect to have kids one day. You've forgotten all those times we joked about Kyle going off to college before we even turned forty, and how much time we'd have to travel and see the world. Now you'll be spending that time changing diapers and warming bottles at two a.m. for your newborn. Your around-the-world trip will come when you're sixty and she's forty...if she hasn't traded you in for a younger man by then."

She shoves the box into my arms and leaves me standing alone in the attic—shocked and dazed. Tammy and I haven't talked about having kids—we've barely talked about what our plans are a week out—but Grace is right. Tammy's very young, and she'll eventually want a baby. If she waits until she's thirty, I'll be retired when our child graduates high school and moves out.

Is that really the life I want? Is that the life I've worked toward all these years?

31

"Dad! Bring the decorations down so we can finish tonight!" Kyle jars me from my visions of experiencing empty-nest syndrome. I move down the attic steps robotically before I push them back up into the ceiling. The one person I'd normally depend on and talk these conundrums through with is the one person I can't turn to for advice now.

Inside the den, I put the box down by the tree. The first ornament Kyle picks up is the same one that drew Grace's eye. He looks at it without speaking for several seconds. The blinking lights on the tree illuminate his face, and I see sadness in his eyes.

"Mom, when I go off to college, can I take this with me?" Kyle looks up at Grace then back down at the picture. "This has always been my favorite picture of us."

"Of course, baby. You can have it." Grace is the only one who can get away with calling him "baby." She has told him he'd always be her baby, regardless of how old he is. Kyle has never once disagreed. Grace hung the moon and stars, in his eyes.

They hang his childhood ornaments as I hand them over. Before long, every hole is filled, and Grace is finally satisfied with the perfect balance on the tree. She settles on the couch to finally rest, and Kyle stretches out on the love seat. I sit next to Grace, against the arm of the couch, and pull her legs into my lap.

She cuts her questioning eyes at me, but I ignore the daggers flying in my direction for touching her without permission. Instead, I slip her shoes and socks off one at a time before I massage her feet and calves.

"You've had a long day, and we gave you more work to do when you got home. I'll make your feet feel better, then you can go shower while I fix dinner. You must be starving."

Holding up my end of the deal is so much harder than I thought it would be. Not because of the acts I have to perform or even because taking care of Grace is a hardship. No, what hurts is when I touch her and I know she hates to feel my caress. What's hard is remembering all the years I wished Grace would look at me the way Tammy does now. What cuts is knowing we're both putting on an elaborate act that only delays our inevitable demise as a couple.

What's impossible is knowing I couldn't change anything even if I wanted to.

Even if tried.

Even if I gave my all.

Grace would never want me again.

~

Grace

"OVER THE PAST TWO WEEKS, Blake has played his part and kept his word. I've checked our cell phone bill but haven't found any texts or calls. Today, I've decided not to look anymore. Whatever he decides to do will happen, regardless if I know right away or not. If I'm honest with myself, I wanted to catch him so I could end this charade between us. Because the nicer he is to me, the more thoughtful he acts, the more it hurts me."

"You still love him." Leigh sits back in her chair, crosses her arms, and narrows her eyes at me. "How can you still love him?"

"I still love the man I used to know. Kyle's father. This Blake isn't that man anymore. But I see glimpses of him sometimes, and it reminds me of what I've lost. All the years with my high school love that have been flushed down the toilet. That makes me mad and hurts at the same time."

"You know…" Leigh draws out the suspense by drawing out those two syllables. "You wouldn't have such a strong reaction to all this if you didn't care about your marriage at all anymore."

"He has a young girlfriend he wants a forever life with, Leigh. He's been making plans to leave me to be with her for a while now. That's not the kind of thing I can just forget. It's hard enough playing pretend for Kyle's sake."

"But it's not all for Kyle's sake. Is it, Grace?"

I pick up my coffee and take a long sip. The longer I avoid eye contact and refuse to acknowledge her question, the more likely she is to drop it.

"I'm not suggesting you should suddenly develop amnesia. I'm simply saying there's no shame in making your marriage work if that's what you both want. My advice is for both of you to have a deep, heart-to-heart talk and commit to what you want to do. He fucked up, I'm not saying he didn't. But this act has you all confused and feeling shit for him you don't want to admit. I don't want to see you hurt again the day after Kyle leaves."

"You think Blake and I could move past this, Leigh?"

"My parents did—and their marriage is stronger because they made it a priority. They weren't afraid to admit where they'd gone wrong, and they fixed it. You and Blake would both have to take a long, hard look in the mirror and move forward together. Do you think you can forgive him?"

Can I? That's the million-dollar question.

"After I first found out about Tammy, I was so hurt and mad and humiliated and alone. It made me crazy to think about the two of them together. To think he was showering her with the attention he denied me. So, when he was on one of his business trips, quote unquote, I checked up on him. He was with her.

"So, I got dressed up and went out to a bar. I was looking to get picked up, and I didn't care who knew it. This handsome, well-dressed man slid up to the bar beside me. He was drinking bourbon neat—told the bartender exactly which brand he wanted and how many fingers. He was sexy and successful and only in town for a couple of days on business.

"I tried to go through with it—I really did. The man kissed like it was an art. His hands heated my body temperature to boiling. The way he looked at me made me believe he'd eat me alive and relish every second of it.

"And that's what stopped me cold.

34

"I realized that's how my husband looked at another woman. The things that stranger made me feel were what my husband made another woman feel. The intimate moments she had with my husband should have been mine all along. Those thoughts chilled my blood, and I rushed out of his hotel room with a mumbled apology."

Leigh stares at me, dumbfounded and speechless. "You never told me about that. Wow."

"I know. It was a hard wake-up call for me and not something I'm proud of doing. Even knowing what Blake was doing, I couldn't go through with it. I couldn't make myself let another man have me. But I also had to face how that stranger made me feel—when he wooed me, when he looked at me, and when he touched me. I haven't had that with Blake in so long...but he hasn't had that from me either."

"Wait—you're not turning into one of those Stockholm syndrome wives who blames themselves for their husband's affairs, are you? Because if you are, I'll kick your ass right now."

Damn, I love my best friend. "No, nothing like that. The cheating is all on him. But I have to accept my faults and how I may have pushed him away. It takes two to stay married, so what did I not do, or not do enough? How did I contribute to the death of our marriage? I can't put all of the blame on him. We obviously had problems before he brought her into the mix."

We finish our break and head back to the unit to do the next round of medications and vitals on our patients. Our conversation keeps replaying in my head, forcing me to take an honest inventory of my shortcomings, his shortcomings, and how our mutual failures played off the other. I am still crushed by his actions, but a small part of me understands his needs weren't being met by me any more than mine were being met by him. He just found someone else who was willing to try a little harder in the areas he needed most, and he let her in.

I was more comfortable with the status quo and thought we'd

always be together. Till death do us part. Isn't that what we vowed?

Since he has made an honest attempt to be a better husband in Kyle's eyes, it's only fair that I step up to the plate and give my all too. For the next eight and a half months anyway. On my way home after my last twelve-hour shift ends, an unsettling truth hits me.

I don't even know what Blake wants or needs to genuinely make him happy. Shouldn't I know that about my husband?

When I get home, I find Blake and Kyle standing in the front yard, in the cold and darkness of our early winter and shorter days, admiring their work again. Kyle meets me at my car, opens my door, and impatiently waits for me to collect my things and get out.

"What are you up to?" I ask with a smile.

"I helped Dad cook dinner. Come try it. We grilled hamburgers and made French fries."

"You grilled out in this weather?"

"Yeah," Kyle laughs and glances over at his dad. "We also tried to make s'mores on the grill, but I say we just need to build a fire pit in the backyard and go all out."

My son is a genius. Blake has mentioned wanting a fire pit many times over the years, but something else always took precedence over building our backyard oasis. No time like the present to rectify that—even if the landscapers think I'm crazy for scheduling the construction in the winter.

"By all means, lead me to the food. Sounds delicious. After we eat, do you two want to take a walk around the neighborhood and look at Christmas lights? Our neighbors may have more lights up than we do. You never know."

"If they do, then we accept their challenge. What do you say, Kyle?"

"Oh, they're going down. No one out-Christmas-lights us."

A little prodding in the right area, with a little threat of competition, and they're both ready to go to battle.

"Are you sure you're not too tired tonight, Mom?"

"No, I'm fine, baby. I wouldn't miss it for the world."

Kyle points out which patties he was specifically responsible for cooking, so I make sure to take one of his. He's proud of his small achievement, and I'm proud of how he's devouring the extra time he has spent with his dad. These small, simple acts give me hope for their relationship in the future.

Blake approaches me after dinner when we're bundling up for our walk in the chilly night air. He helps slide on my coat and speaks, keeping his voice low so Kyle doesn't overhear.

"Are you sure you're up for this tonight? You've been going in a lot more lately, and you just finished a long shift. We can go tomorrow night if you'd rather wait."

"No, I'm fine to go for a walk. It'll be nice to get outside. I've been stuck inside too long."

"Okay, if you're sure. There's something we need to discuss when we get back."

Did he find the letter while they were cooking? Is that why he wants to talk? I know that's an irrational fear talking since they had no reason to get the flour out for hamburgers and fries. Thoughts swirl and my mind races, considering the different reasons we'd need to "talk" now. My mind bounces from the routine household chores to the life-altering decision to end our façade. Then I put that aside because surely he wouldn't join in on the Christmas lights competition if that were the case.

Since I already have more than enough bullshit cluttering my mind, I refocus and put a smile on my face.

"All right, Blake. Is everything okay?"

"Nothing's wrong, but there is something I need to tell you. I don't want it to affect our family stroll, so let's wait until we get back."

"Fair enough. Ready to go?"

He nods and meets my gaze. Our eyes lock, and I read sadness in his. He looks lost—trapped between what he wants to do and what he knows he should do. Part of me thinks I should release him from his promises and let the chips fall where they may. But I can't. For Kyle's sake, we can both sacrifice what we want for a short time.

"So, Mom. First, I'm glad you changed out of your scrubs because that wind is cold. Second, I should tell you...we didn't really cook the hamburgers. We bought them and just warmed them up on the grill. But we did try the s'mores thing."

I wrap my arm around Kyle's waist when we start to walk and look up at my boy—the one who's taller than me now. "Yeah, I know, Kyle. I recognized the seasoning and happen to know we don't have any. But it's the thought that counts, and I appreciate you two having dinner ready."

"Do you appreciate it enough to buy the new football video game for me?"

"Do you still believe in Santa, Kyle?" Blake asks teasingly.

"Santa and the Easter Bunny if it gets me that game," he quips.

Our combined laughter carries on the breeze, and my cold heart thaws a little more in spite of the temperature. We walk at a leisurely pace, admiring the lights and ingenuity of our neighbors. Blake and Kyle take note of the best displays and plot how to beat them. Over the couple of hours that we stroll, talk, and laugh, I catch Blake staring at me several times.

I wish I could read his mind.

But as soon as Kyle retreats to his room, I don't have to wish anymore. Blake asks me to sit in the den with him so we can have that talk.

"I'm only telling you this because I'm trying to be honest and hold up my pledge to you. I'm not telling you this to hurt you."

"Okay. Go on." I inhale a deep breath and slowly release it. I have a feeling I won't like what he has to say.

"Tammy called me today. I answered to tell her not to call me again until Kyle leaves for college. She said she misses me and doesn't understand why it has to be this way. So I explained it to her again and asked her to be more supportive of my decision to focus on Kyle during this time. She didn't like it, but she agreed. I just wanted to tell you up front so you don't think I'm hiding anything from you."

CHAPTER 5

Blake

"Tell me the truth, Blake. Not what you think I want to hear. Take everything off the table. If you had your choice right now, would you still be here with your son, or would you take off to be with her?"

A few weeks ago, my truthful answer would've been much different. Tonight, I know without a shadow of a doubt what my answer is. Walking around the neighborhood with Grace and Kyle, I had to face how selfish I've become over the years. I've been so consumed with myself, I didn't even notice how much they'd suffered because of my focus on work and career and money, when all they wanted was a little more of my time and attention. Taking the time to put everything on the back burner—including my own ego—I realized something incredibly profound.

My need to feel important, worthy, and desired can only be satisfied by these two people. No outsider can fill that gaping hole inside of me. Not Tammy. Not my boss. Not being accepted by Grace's parents.

I've realized something else in my time apart from Tammy. Without the thrill of forbidden love driving my decisions, I can look at my relationship with her more objectively and be honest with myself. For once.

It was never about her. It was never about falling in love with her or not being able to live without her. My relationship with Tammy was born from missing what Grace and I once had—and my stupidity in looking for that deep relationship elsewhere. The truth is, I don't want Tammy. I was in love with the *idea* of her— how she wanted me, how she looked at me, how she needed me. Most of all, how all of that combined made me feel like less of a failure.

But I was a fool.

I wanted her to be Grace. I wanted Grace to feel that way toward me again, to not want to leave my side, to be in love with me.

"I'd be right here, building my relationship with Kyle. You were right to give me this ultimatum. Over the past couple of weeks, I've spent so much time with him—just getting to know him again. We're reconnecting, and I wouldn't trade that for anything."

She stands and begins to walk away then stops. She turns her head and looks over her shoulder at me. "Thank you for being honest. I've had a long day, so I'm going up to bed now."

My eyes stay glued to her when she walks away and climbs the stairs to the bedroom we used to share. The conversation with Tammy didn't go quite as smoothly as I alluded, but I didn't feel right about getting into the details because of the accusations Tammy made about Grace.

"She's just doing this to control you, Blake, and you're letting her. She only wants to keep us apart," Tammy cried, pulling my heart and mind in different directions.

"You're wrong about her."

"No, I'm not. She wants you for herself. She's trying to push me out

of your life. I know women, Blake. This is her plan. Don't let her do this to us."

"I've told you—this will be over in a few months. It's not that long to wait for me. I'm waiting for you."

"You're not sleeping with her, then?"

"No, I'm not."

"I still don't trust her. This will all backfire on you. Mark my words because when it happens, I'll scream 'I told you so' from the rooftops."

"This is the last time I'll explain this to you, so you'd better listen up, Tammy. Grace is not manipulating me to get me to stay with her. This is all for our son, and Grace is right. She's right to ask this of me. She's right to demand it. She's right to expect it. Our divorce will be hard enough on Kyle when the time comes, but he deserves to have a happy, carefree senior year until then. Once he's out of the house, it won't be such a culture shock for him. This is happening whether you like it or not. If you can't live with this for eight more months, then I have to question if you love me at all."

"I do love you, Blake. I'm sorry."

"Don't call anymore until you hear from me. I'm not going to screw this up."

"All right," she sniffed, defeated. "I still feel like you're changing. Like this is the end of us."

When I hung up, I leaned back in my chair and stared at my phone, wondering when the exact moment was that I stopped missing Tammy. I couldn't tell Tammy I also felt like it was the end of our relationship. Not because I wanted to hold on to her, but because I don't want her to show up here and cause a scene in front of Kyle. I'd lose all the respect he has for me now. That can't happen, not with us finally rebuilding our relationship.

Her presence would only hurt Grace too, and I won't allow that. After peering into small windows of the time when she and I were truly one, I know exactly what's been missing from my life.

When did my selfish needs finally fall below the happiness of my family? And why did it take so damn long? When did saving my family become so important to me?

I finally realize the obvious truth. When I put my focus, my attention, and my energy into loving and providing for my family, everything else fades into the background. When I look at Grace, I see the woman I've always burned for, the one I've always loved. She's the one I should've held on to as if my life depended on it—because it does. Grace can't be replaced with someone who makes me feel good about myself in the short term; the thoughts and feelings of being a failure will return. Only, they'll be worse knowing I've also failed Grace and Kyle. Exchanging the life we've built for something unknown won't suddenly make me a new man.

How could I have been so stupid and blind all this time?

Now I'm watching my wife retreat to the bed alone and wishing we could just have an open, honest conversation about what we both want. What we're feeling. What we're doing. So why can't I? Why can't I just climb those stairs, barge into our bedroom, and tell my wife what I want?

Because I don't deserve her.

Because I haven't atoned for my sins yet.

Because I'm still learning to be the man she needs.

Because I don't know if she can ever love me again.

Because I don't know if I'm worth the pain I've caused her.

So, I turn on the TV and flip through the channels instead. With my shoes kicked off and my clothes in a heap on the floor, I stretch out on the couch in my lounge pants. A thick blanket covers me, the fire in the fireplace warms me, and the low murmur of voices lulls me to sleep.

But it's a fitful sleep—full of disturbing dreams with heartbreak and disappointments. When I wake, I'm more exhausted than ever, and more aggravated. My dreams all told me one thing —Grace will never want me again. In the shower, I decide if I'm going down in flames, I'll go down fighting tooth and nail, and no fucking dream will decide my destiny.

It's time to show Grace and Kyle exactly the husband and father I should've been the entire time. It's time to prove to myself that I'm better than what I've allowed myself to become. Grace wants me to pretend to be the best father and husband I can be to help Kyle? She'll get more than she bargained for because I'm done with the pretending part.

I'll do whatever I have to do to make her fall in love with me again. One day at a time. Step by step.

I at least have to give this my best attempt—all three of us deserve that chance. A new beginning...a fresh start to make our family what it never has been before. Rock solid. Presents won't solve our problems, I know that. But with Christmas only a week away, I want to find the perfect way to express my apology and my promise for the future.

"Where are you off to today?" Grace asks when I enter the kitchen fully dressed. It's Saturday morning, and she's at the stove cooking breakfast. Kyle sits at the table, sleepy-eyed and with crazy bed hair, but his expression tells me he enjoys this scene.

"I have a few errands to run today, but I shouldn't be gone long."

Her smile falters, and sadness overtakes her features. She doesn't trust me, and I don't blame her. She automatically assumes my errands involve Tammy.

"Kyle, do you want to go with me?"

"Where are you going?"

"Probably to the mall."

"You are voluntarily going to the mall? Who are you, and what have you done with my dad? He would never go unless there were blackmail pictures involved."

"Smartass," I chuckle and playfully swat at his arm. Leaning down so only he can hear me, I whisper, "I have an idea for your mom's present. Don't you need to get her something too?"

"Oh, yeah. I do," he whispers back. "Mom, I'm going with Dad today. You can't come, though."

"Of course I can." She grins mischievously. I've missed that playful twinkle in her eyes. "I have my own car. I can drive it and everything."

"Fine. You can go with us, but you can't look," Kyle compromises.

"You two go ahead. I'll call Leigh and get her to go with me. Maybe we can meet for lunch later."

"A lunch date with my wife?" I wink at her. "I'll take you up on that offer."

After breakfast, Kyle speeds through his shower while I help Grace with the dishes. My fingers brush against hers, and the brief contact hits me like a bolt of lightning. The desire I once thought was dead is back in full force. Grace's eyes jerk up to meet mine. Her lips are parted, and her face is flushed. She feels it too. I know she does.

"Ready, Dad?"

Kyle's timing is perfect. His entrance saves me from making a fatal mistake. Had I gone with my gut instinct and kissed her, I would've ruined all my plans. I won't rush this. I'll take my time and convince her to fall in love with me one romantic gesture at a time.

My eyes stay connected to Grace's when I answer Kyle. "Yes, I am ready. Now that I'm clear on what I need."

"Perfect," he replies, unaware of the underlying meaning in my words. "You can help me figure out what I need to get."

"Have fun," Grace says as we're walking out.

I stop and turn to face her. "You sure you're okay going with Leigh? You're welcome to come with us."

"I'm fine. You two go do your thing. I'll do mine, and we'll catch up early this afternoon."

I nod and give her a small smile. So many words on the tip of my tongue and so many things to say. But I swallow them down and wait for the right time. Whenever that may be.

"Are we really going to the mall?" Kyle asks when I slide behind the wheel.

"Yes. Well, maybe around the mall. The best jewelry store is just across the parking lot from the mall entrance."

"Do you already know what you're getting her?"

"I have a good idea."

"Any chance we can swing getting her a pair of diamond earrings from me? I've heard her tell Leigh that she'll get a pair one day. Eventually. But she never splurges on herself, so I don't know how she plans to get them."

With a smile and a nod, I apparently make Kyle's day. The beaming grin on his face makes me proud. He loves his mother, and he's not ashamed to show it. When we walk into the jewelry store, the young woman behind the front counter looks up and holds my gaze with a bat of her eyelashes. She smiles warmly and shifts her stance to fully face me. The signs are so obvious, but I ignore her open invitation.

"Hello. How can I help you today?" she purrs.

"I'm looking for a ring for my wife." I keep my expression passive, but the inflection in my voice leaves no doubt regarding my intentions.

"And a pair of diamond earrings too," Kyle adds.

"Of course." She slips into professional mode without a hitch. "What type of ring do you have in mind?"

"A Past, Present, and Future ring."

She shows me to the case with the options and leaves me to look at them while she shows Kyle to the earrings. My eyes scan over the rows of rings until I spot the perfect set. Three round-cut stones in platinum and a matching band with wraparound diamonds is exactly what I had in mind. Visions of renewing our vows in the future bounce in my mind.

Though it's not something I could pull off in a week—or even that Grace would want it that soon—maybe she'll be ready to forgive me by spring. After I've given her every reason to love me again. After I've shown her I want to be the kind of husband she needs. After I prove I'll move heaven and earth to give her the big wedding we never had, if that's what she wants. If she forgives me. If she even wants me back.

I have to face the very real possibility that scenario may never happen.

Kyle steps up beside me with a satisfied expression on his face. "It looks like you found a pair you like for her?"

"Yes, she'll be thrilled. She deserves them. She's done so much for me my whole life. But after all this stuff with applying to colleges and helping me pick majors, she deserves sainthood."

My heart drops to my feet. I didn't even know they'd been working so hard on any of that. I've been so wrapped up in myself, I've neglected my entire family and everything that's important to them. This is time I'll never get back, memories I'll never be part of in Kyle's life. I should kick my own ass.

The salesgirl opens the velvet box to show me the pair Kyle selected, and I'm in awe. Round-cut diamond studs that match the ring set perfectly. "Beautiful, Kyle. They're perfect." I point to the wedding set, and the girl retrieves them from the case.

"These are a size six," she says and hands them to me.

"Those are the ones, Dad. Get those." Kyle's eyes never leave the rings when he speaks, and I think fate has just made the final decision for me. "She'll love them."

"That's her size. I'll take them." I check my watch and realize we have plenty of time left before Grace and Leigh will be ready to meet us for lunch. "As much as this hurts me to ask, do you want to go to the mall and look for a present for your girlfriend?"

"Yeah, let's get it over with before the crowd gets worse. I've kinda waited till the last minute, huh?"

"You and me both, son."

CHAPTER 6

Grace

"They're leaving. Can you get your cousin and his guys over here now?" Even though I'm alone, I whisper into the phone, begging Leigh to help me out.

"You know, for someone who doesn't love her husband anymore, you're going out of your way to surprise him with this."

"Stop giving me shit and call your cousin, Leigh. Right now!"

She's laughing when I hang up on her and rush to take my shower. I have a text from her when I get out, letting me know the landscaping crew will be in my backyard within thirty minutes to start working on a patio and fire pit. The area is relatively small, but it'll take the crew all day to complete the work.

I just have to keep Blake and Kyle away long enough to give the workers time to finish the job. We've already covered the basics—I sent her cousin a picture of what I want and a picture of my current space. Leigh will oversee the rest of the details for me while I meet my guys for an early afternoon lunch and hopefully a matinee to delay our return home.

Leigh arrives as I'm rushing out the door, and I grab her in a tight embrace. "Thank you. You're a lifesaver."

"I want you to be happy, Grace. Whatever that means, I support you."

"I know you do. I just don't know what it means myself right now. All I can do is focus on getting Kyle into the college he wants the most. If I try to deal with anything else, it just overwhelms me. One crisis at a time is all I can handle right now."

"I'm afraid you don't have that luxury, my friend. But I'll do what I can and what you need to help you through it."

I love her, but sometimes I hate it when she's right.

On my way toward the mall, I start to call Kyle to find out where they are and ask if it's safe for me to join them yet. Then I stop and decide to call Blake instead. I can't use Kyle as our middleman, and a "normal" wife would call her husband anyway.

He sounds surprised when he answers, and I almost laugh out loud. "Grace? Is everything okay?"

"Yes, everything's fine. Leigh couldn't join me today, so I'm heading out alone. Are you two finished conspiring?"

"We are," he chuckles. "We're shopping for Kyle's girlfriend now. Why don't you join us?"

"Sounds like fun. I should be there in about twenty minutes."

We agree on a place to meet since the mall is packed with all the last-minute procrastinators. When I circle the parking lot, I see Blake standing on the curb. He jogs over to me, dodging frantic shoppers and little old ladies not watching where they're going.

"I'll park the car for you. I don't want you walking out here alone." He opens my door and waits for me to get out. I've never met this Blake before, and my heart squeezes from the gesture. The man I married was fun and witty, but we were both too young to realize what true romance was. These small acts mean so much—opening doors, parking the car, showing how he wants to take care of me. Where would we be had this been our relationship all along?

When I stand, we're close—so close my chest brushes against his, and the friction sends electrical charges exploding throughout my body. Ignoring my feelings is becoming harder when he does thoughtful things like this. Then I remind myself "act" is the appropriate word. I'm not the one he's in love with anymore.

The acts I take as caring are only that—acts. He's playing a part for Kyle, to teach him how to treat a woman. Does he do all of this for *her*?

This isn't even a simple problem of miscommunication. He was honest about Tammy calling him, but he didn't tell her it was over between them. He just reiterated that his reason for being here is Kyle—reestablishing and building his relationship with his son. Doing the same for his relationship with his wife isn't even on his radar. The sooner I burn that fact into my brain, the better off I'll be.

When I join Kyle just inside the entrance, he puts his big arm around my shoulders and pulls me into his side. In a sea of storms and out of control waves, he's my anchor. We've always been close, and part of him worries about leaving me to start his own life. He's protective of me, and I appreciate his concern, but I want him to be an independent young man who isn't afraid to stand on his own two feet. That's how I've raised him.

"Have you found your girlfriend anything yet?"

"No." He shakes his head and rolls his eyes. "You women use so much shit. I don't even know where to start."

"Start with perfume and purses, Kyle. Perfume and purses."

"I'm not carrying a purse through the mall."

"It'll be in a bag, son."

"I don't care. You pick it out, and you carry it. I'll carry everything else you want to buy."

Blake joins us after finally finding a parking spot. "Kyle, why don't you drive my car home, and I'll drive your mom? I had to park all the way at the end of the row, and I'm not letting her walk alone in this madhouse."

"Sure, Dad." Kyle casts a quick glance at me and lifts his eyebrow to confirm it's okay.

What does he know?

"That's fine with me. I like having a chauffeur."

I purposely take them to every store in the mall that carries purses and perfume. When enough time has passed and I know they're at their breaking point, I finally pick out the gifts and even throw in a matching wallet for extra girlfriend brownie points. Much to Kyle's relief, I take them to the restaurant and sit down to have a late lunch.

"I think Dad and I are better at this shopping thing than you are. We knew exactly what we wanted and where to get it, and we wasted no time checking out. Efficient. Decisive. Smart shoppers. That's us."

"I'm sure you are," I reply with a sly grin.

Kyle narrows his eyes at me for a moment before his bottom jaw drops open. "I can't believe you. Betrayed by my own mother."

"What are you talking about, Kyle?" Blake asks, and I giggle.

"Dad, I hate to break it to you, but Mom completely just played us. She knew all along what she was going to get, but she dragged us to every store in the mall on purpose."

Blake slowly turns his head to look at me, and I feign an overly innocent expression. "I'm sure I have no idea what you're talking about, Kyle. Now, after we eat, I think we should go to the four o'clock movie and treat ourselves. We've earned it after a hard day of shopping."

Kyle folds his arms over his chest and arches one eyebrow. "You're not fooling me."

"It's a Marvel movie."

"We're going," they both reply, and I smile triumphantly.

It'll be dark by the time we get home, making my surprise even more perfect. Cold night, warm fire, roasting marshmallows, and making s'mores over our new fire pit while the snow flurries around us.

Romantic and heartbreaking at the same time.

Blake stands in line to get our concessions while Kyle and I save our seats. With all the glances Kyle has given me, I know he can't wait to get me alone so he can confirm his suspicions.

"What have you done?" he asks the moment we're seated.

I pull up a picture on my phone and show him our new backyard haven. "Think your dad will like it?"

"He'll love it, Mom. You did good. I can't wait to see it and use it myself. Although, I'm a little peeved you waited until just before I go off to college before you had it built."

"Yes, that was my plan all along. Wait until the very last minute so you couldn't enjoy it at all. You caught me."

He chuckles with me. "Maybe I'll surprise you and come home more often than you think I will."

"If you think that's punishing me, then, by all means, you should come home every weekend."

Blake climbs the stairs and takes the open seat beside me, putting me between my two guys. I hold the popcorn in my lap, and Blake wraps his arm around my shoulders. I haven't felt the comfort of his embrace in so long, and I desperately want to snuggle into him. Just one more time.

"He's really going to miss you, ya know?" Blake leans in close to talk to me. His lips brush against the shell of my ear. His deep voice reverberates through me, the ripples flowing like a current straight to my core.

"Huh?" I blurt out obtusely, because my brain seems to have taken a leave of absence.

"Kyle. He'll miss you when he leaves. He's mentioned a couple of times how he hates that his top-pick college is so far away. Don't be surprised if he goes to a closer school instead."

"I won't let him do that. He knows better. I want what's best for him and what makes him happy. He shouldn't even consider me when he picks a college," I whisper back. Kyle has worked too hard for his perfect GPA and the high scores on admissions tests to settle for anything less than exactly what he wants. I won't be the cause of him giving up his dream.

"Maybe being close to home and spending time with his family is what makes him happy. Maybe that's exactly what he wants and needs, only he didn't realize it until now."

The intimate timbre of his voice makes me turn and stare into his eyes until the theater lights dim to darkness. I'm not sure we're talking about Kyle and what he wants anymore. This suddenly feels like we've moved on to something else entirely.

Am I ready to hear that from Blake, though?

~

Blake

GRACE DIDN'T OBJECT to my arm being around her during the movie. She didn't flinch or pull away. Was it just hopeful thinking on my part to believe she actually moved closer to me?

The day we spent together was the best day I've had in a long time. Despite the crowds of rude shoppers. Regardless of the number of stores she dragged us into. No matter how many purses we looked at—that looked exactly the same as the ones we looked at in the previous stores. The difference was Grace. She was funny and goofy and full of life.

I know she kept us out all day for a reason, though I still don't know why. If her motive was simply to spend time with Kyle and me, I'll take it. If she only wanted to spend time with Kyle and my presence was a by-product, I'll take that too, because that gives me a chance to prove the ways I'm changing, the ways I've changed. Every chance I get, I'll do my best to turn this nightmare we've been living in back into a dream.

"Thank you for getting the car. I could've walked with you, though."

"Not with all these people and terrible drivers everywhere. They'd run over you to snatch that bag out of your hand."

Her laughter fills the car, and it is music to my ears. We're alone, and she's laughing. I have hope for us. "You're probably right about that. Christmas shopping gets harder every year."

"Maybe, but just so you know, I've thoroughly enjoyed today."

"Even when I made you model different color purses so I could see how they looked?" She cuts her eyes over to me, that playful gleam of hers shining brightly in them.

"Even then. The people walking by got a laugh out of it too."

"You got a round of applause when you took your catwalk stroll. I was impressed." She belly-laughs at the memory, then turns solemn when she continues. "I should've videoed that."

The change in her tone concerns me. She went from laughing to sad in a split second. All I know is I need to turn this conversation back around to focus on the fun we had together.

"Maybe we'll get lucky and someone else did, then it'll show up on Facebook or YouTube." My deadpan tone does the trick, and her smile is back in full force.

"Wouldn't it be great if you went viral?"

"Oh yes. That would be just perfect."

"Blake, I enjoyed spending the day with you and Kyle, too. Nothing about this is easy, but I see the effort you're making, and I want you to know I appreciate it. Kyle does too. I can tell. He still spends time with his friends and girlfriend—I never expected that to change—but now he wants to spend time with you too. That's what's important."

"You're right, of course. I've seen the change in our relationship with the time he and I have spent together. But that's not all that's important, Grace. I've realized so much in the past few weeks, I can barely believe it myself. Do you feel it too?"

I turn into our driveway and put the car into park. When I

turn to Grace, tears drop from her eyes onto her cheeks. She quickly wipes them away, but more take their place. This is all my fault—the pain I've caused her, the damage I've done to our marriage, the time with her I've taken for granted. I desperately want to make it all up to her. If she'll let me. If she'll have me.

A knock on my window startles me, and I jerk my head toward the noise. Kyle stands by the car, bouncing up and down on his toes in excitement with a huge grin covering his face. When I roll down the window, Grace turns her face away to dry her eyes.

"Dad, you gotta come see what Mom has done. I knew she was up to something today."

Grace chuckles from beside me. "You need to quit snooping, you tattletale!"

"Like I could miss it even if I tried. Come on, Dad. You're gonna love it."

Kyle trots off around the corner of the house toward the backyard, and I turn back to Grace. "Can we finish this conversation later? Please?"

"Yes, we can talk about it. But you have to consider my feelings on this, Blake. You've been seeing someone else for six months behind my back. You had plans to divorce me and be with your new soul mate. Three weeks of pretending to care about me is hardly enough to make me believe you've suddenly changed. We both need more time to be sure of what we want and what our next move will be."

"Grace, I don't need another second to know for sure what I want. I'm willing to give you the rest of my life if that's how much time you need to decide for yourself."

A sob breaks free, and she drops her chin to her chest.

She wants to believe me, but she's afraid to give me a chance. But that's okay, I have to earn her trust and love again. At least now, I don't feel like I need to restrain my feelings. The only way to convince her is to show her—every minute of every day.

She quickly regains her composure and wipes her face again. "We'd better join Kyle before he drags us out of the car."

I jump out and jog around the car to open her door. She looks up at me, confusion covering her beautiful face, and I smile sheepishly. "Step one of my 'Win Grace Back' campaign is to spoil you."

"Stop making me cry," she chuckles and whisks away a teardrop.

"You'll only have happy tears from now on." I take her hand and help her stand, then wrap my arm around her as we walk toward the back of the house.

When we turn the corner, my legs stop moving, and my mouth drops open. "Grace. Sweetheart. What did you do?"

"Merry Christmas, a few days early. I wanted to surprise you. You've wanted to do this for a long time, but something else always got in the way or had to be done first. I hope you still like this design."

"It's perfect." My arm tightens around her, and my chest swells with gratitude when I feel her arm slide around my waist to return the embrace.

We walk closer to the new stone-paver patio, complete with bench seating around the raised fire pit in the center. A fire is already going, casting a warm glow across the snow-covered lawn. Adirondack chairs are placed around the perimeter, and small tables with hurricane lamps sit between the chairs.

Kyle is already kicked back in one of the chairs, a shit-eating grin splitting his face in two. He lifts his arm and holds up a box wrapped with shiny red foil and a huge silver bow. "This has your name on it, Dad. Maybe you should open it now."

Grace's lips lift as she shrugs one shoulder. "You can open it, but if Kyle sees what's inside, you may lose it."

"We'll see about that." I take the box from Kyle and sit in the chair next to him to open it. When I see the contents, I can't help but laugh. "S'mores over a real fire tonight!"

"Yes! Give me that box," Kyle demands.

After I hand him the box, I look at Grace and pat my leg. "Come sit with us and have dessert. Kyle, your mom gets the first one."

Even though I put her on the spot, she takes a seat on my leg, and I pull her against my chest. She lays her head on my shoulder, and it occurs to me that I'd be happy to stay just like this—with my wife in my arms and our son by my side. Enjoying our home. Laughing with each other. Treasuring what matters.

While Kyle opens the bags to put Grace's s'more together, I whisper my heart's desire to her. "I know we'll be busy with Christmas parties and dinners over the next week, but I'd really like to take you out after the holiday. What do you say, Grace? Will you go out on a date with me?"

"Yes, I will," she replies. "But don't expect me to go dutch or to put out on the first date."

Her sense of humor was one of the first things I loved about her. I never realized how much I've missed it until just now.

"What are we doing for Christmas this year? Are Gran and Pops coming over?" Kyle asks, referring to my parents.

"Yeah, we always spend time with Jeffrey and Anna. They're such wonderful people," Grace says. "But we're going to my parents' house Christmas Eve."

Kyle and I both freeze. I don't think I'm even breathing.

"Why would we do that, Mom?" Kyle puts the chocolate and marshmallows down then crosses his arms over his chest. "They treat you like shit. At least, they did the last time I saw them, which was forever ago. I'm a lot bigger now. I will kick their asses if they pull that again."

"Get in line, son. If you remember, they called the cops on me," I add.

"We need to go and try to make amends if we can." Grace stares off into the flames, not meeting our disbelieving stares. Then I realize she isn't doing it on purpose—she's lost deep in thought.

"Why do they treat us so bad?" Kyle asks.

"Because Grace was pregnant with you during her senior year of high school, and her parents didn't approve of me. They still don't, to this day. Your mom had to move in to my parents' house and finish high school. Then we got married, and that really set them off. Her parents didn't speak to her again until you were seven. That's when we went over there and ended up in a fight with them again. That's also the reason she's seen them *maybe* a handful of times since then," I explain.

Gretchen and Matt Baldwin are not my favorite people.

Kyle moves in front of us and kneels in front of Grace. "Mom, tell me what's going on."

"They're getting older, Kyle. If we don't have a relationship with them now, we never will."

Kyle's eyes narrow, and his brows draw down. With his hand covering his mouth, he draws his fingers across his cheeks and studies his mom. His brain is working overtime at this unexpected announcement. Grace reaches up and pulls his hand from his face and holds it in hers.

"You're too young to worry yourself like this, Kyle. If they're assholes, we'll just leave. No reason to get all worked up. Maybe they've mellowed in their golden years." She tries to soothe him, but he isn't buying it.

"I know you as well as you know me, Mom. You don't believe that. If they had, we would've heard from them before now."

"Maybe. But doesn't everyone deserve a second chance?"

She's got me there. I can't argue—but I can protect her at all costs.

CHAPTER 7

Grace

*B*lake is still sleeping on the couch, but we stay up later and later each night. With Kyle out of school for winter break, spending time with Blake is easier. There's less pressure on us while we wade through the murky waters of our marriage with Kyle around as a buffer. Blake seems sincere when he compliments me, whispers sweet words like he used to do long ago, and flirts with me.

But my heart is torn. The betrayal is so hard to move past. I'd mourned our marriage when I first learned about Tammy. I cried, I screamed, I threw our pictures and shattered the frames into millions of pieces—jagged edges that matched the remnants of my heart. Then I sought out a counselor to help me face the future. The changes, the uncertainty, and the inevitable days when I'd think all was lost.

I was ready to face loneliness. Hopelessness. Sadness.

Now he's pushing me to the verge of hope again. I don't know if I can take the disappointment if he fails me again. Though she'd never say, "I told you so," my counselor did warn me this could happen.

"What if you learn you're still in love with your husband?" she asked.

"No way," I insisted. *"That man is not the man I fell in love with or the man I married. I'm only concerned about Kyle. For my son, I'll endure the nausea looking at Blake causes me now."*

"You're walking a fine line, Grace. I just want you to be prepared either way."

At that time, I thought I was ready. Ready to let go and move on. Ready to let him have his happily ever after with her, knowing she'd soon leave him for someone else. Then he went and threw this curveball at me, making me care about him again. Making me feel as concerned for his future as I am Kyle's.

"Mom, do we have to go?"

"For the hundredth time, yes. Now, grab their presents from under the tree, and let's go."

The tension in the car is thick as we drive to my parents' house. It was never inviting to begin with. It felt more like a museum—cold, quiet, and unfeeling. No life to be found or felt, only priceless belongings that were more important than the people forced to live there. I doubt much has changed for the better—but I have to try.

Blake parks in their driveway and turns his face to me, the engine still running. "Are you sure you want to do this? We can still leave if you want."

"Look, guys, I don't really want to be here any more than you do. Let's try to make the best of it and see what happens."

Blake and Kyle flank me on the front porch, and I ring the doorbell. The chimes echo throughout the enormous house. The housekeeper opens the door and shows us to the library. The tree is professionally decorated, and expensive Christmas trinkets line the mantle over the fireplace. Along the tops of the bookshelves, lighted houses create an idyllic scene.

"Make yourselves comfortable. Mr. and Mrs. Baldwin will be

right with you," the housekeeper says then closes the door behind her.

Perfect. They have to make a grand entrance and remind us of our place—the one beneath them. Kyle steps behind me, and I sense him go into protective mode. Then Blake moves closer beside me and takes my hand in his.

"We'll do this together, Grace. If it gets too hard for you, I'll take the brunt of their resentment myself."

"They don't mean shit to me. If they start on my mom, I'll give them a piece of my mind they'll never forget. Neither of you has to do a thing," Kyle adds.

I smile, my heart warmed by the care my guys show for my well-being. But... "Thank you both for looking out for me, but just relax. There's something I need to talk to my mother about in private, so don't start a brawl. If our conversation ends badly, we'll leave and think no more about them."

"You're talking to her alone? Does she know this?" Blake asks, surprised and slightly appalled.

"Yes. I know what you're thinking—she doesn't deserve my time—but this is important to me."

The door opens, and my mother comes sweeping into the room with all her grandeur. For all her pomp and airs, she stops cold when she sees Kyle.

"This can't be—"

"That's Kyle, all right. He's a senior this year," I reply.

"Oh my God." Her hand covers her heart as she realizes how much time has passed, wasted. "I can't believe you've gotten so big."

"Yeah, that's what happens after ten years," he replies.

I don't correct him for speaking to her that way because I want her to understand she can't run over him, and she has no power over him. To my surprise, she simply nods.

"You're right, Kyle. We've been fools. I'd like a chance to get to know you now, though."

"I guess it couldn't hurt. Unless you're mean to my mom. Then all bets are off, and someone will hurt a lot."

"You're obviously protective of her. That's very admirable. She and I have had our differences, but I hope this visit is to put all that behind us."

"It is. It's a chance for all of us to heal and hopefully have a better relationship in the near future," I reply.

"I would love that," my dad says as he enters the room.

The housekeeper announces that dinner is ready, and we file out of the room toward the dining area. We take our seats, and the awkwardness fades away as the food fills our plates and stomachs. Though, the butterflies in my stomach still flutter from just thinking about the conversation I'll soon have with my mother.

After dinner, Blake, Kyle, and Dad retreat to the study, Dad's separate room that could be a cool man cave if Mom would let him redecorate it. It's the only room in the house where Mom allows him to enjoy his pipe. The three of them will play pool and get acquainted while Mom and I sit in the enclosed sunroom to talk alone.

"How have you been, Mom?" I ask when we're seated.

She looks at me thoughtfully, like she's seeing me for the first time. Maybe she is—our interactions have been brief and stilted for years. We've spent almost as much time apart as we have together. "I'm glad you came. I was afraid you wouldn't. I wasn't even sure you'd take my call."

"I was surprised to hear from you."

She nods and seems uncomfortable. "Life has a funny way of knocking you flat on your back when you least expect it."

Don't I know it.

She stands and moves to the window, looking out at the lights and snow. "One of the ladies from my country club just experienced the worst thing I can imagine. She watched her daughter die right in front of her. Another car hit them head on, and they were pinned inside their car. She couldn't move to help her daughter, and her daughter died before they reached the hospital.

"I realize I've wasted a lot of time we could've spent together being angry with you over something so trivial now. Kyle is a wonderful young man, and you and Blake are still happily married after all these years. Despite the odds against you with your young age and starting out with a newborn, you've built a happy home and a wonderful life. I'm so sorry, Grace. We'll never get those years back, but I'd like to make the rest of our lives the best we've ever known."

"I'd like that too, Mom. What about Blake? Are you finally ready to accept and include him in this family?"

"We are. I know you haven't touched your trust fund once in all these years because of your anger toward me. The balance has grown considerably—your father has made sure of that. But we've also set up accounts for Blake and for Kyle, with no stipulations and no strings attached, except that your name is on the accounts along with theirs. All of you will be cared for if you accept it. I'm not trying to buy your forgiveness or your love. I'm simply trying to do what I should've done eighteen years ago."

She walks to the table and picks up three beige envelopes.

"Here are the financial documents for each account. Your father and I arranged it so we have no control or say-so over the money. No hidden power struggle and no games. Just a sincere apology."

I stand and take them from her hand. Then I pull her to me and wrap my arms around her, thankful she offered this olive branch and saved me from having to ask for help in getting Kyle off to college. She starts crying and wraps her arms around me, squeezing me tight. "Thank you for doing this. It means more to me than you know."

We take our seats again and continue chatting, sharing events that we've both missed out on. She seems like a completely different person now, and I can only pray she remains this benevolent in the days to come.

When we walk back inside the house, I slide the documents into my bag and consider how much this gesture will help Kyle while he's away. How much of a burden it relieves from Blake and me. When we rejoin the men, we exchange gifts and have an extra plate of dessert with coffee by the fireplace.

Everything feels so right and peaceful, I almost forget that nothing actually is.

"That went better than I expected," Kyle says on our ride home. "Grandpa is actually a pretty cool old man."

"I agree—and I'm surprised," Blake replies. He turns to look at me before speaking again. "How'd your conversation with your mom go?"

"It was good. She told me why she broke down and called to invite us over." I retold the story of her friend's daughter and how Mom would feel if anything happened to me before we'd made amends.

"So, Mom, since Dad already got his present, what are the chances I can open mine tonight?"

∾

Blake

THE GLIMPSES I've seen of the woman I first fell in love with are more frequent and more potent the more time we spend together. The times I see this side of her, I feel so much the worse about what I've done to us, and I wish so fucking badly I could take it all back. Every last minute of it. There's nothing I want more than to make her forget it all happened—to give her everything I never gave her before. All of my love, all the time, for the rest of our lives.

When did I suddenly realize this? When did I decide I'm in love with her again?

I think I've known all along and tried to fool myself into believing the grass was greener elsewhere. The slower I try to take things and allow our relationship to progress naturally, the harder it is for me to deny my thoughts and feelings. I've been out of our bed for far too long.

But she can't believe my sudden change of heart and direction from only my words and confession. And I don't blame her. If I'd found her with another man, I'd be in jail right now. Trusting her again would be out of the question, and that's part of my hesitation of going all out and telling her how much I love her. It's why I'm not pushing harder for us to be a true couple again just yet.

I know I wouldn't trust her if the roles were reversed, so how can I expect her to trust me again so soon? What kind of relationship can we have with no trust? Or if she's suspicious of me every time I go out of town for work, if she questions my every phone call or text, if she decides I'm not worth the constant worry my infidelity caused her...

Maybe I'm getting way ahead of myself here. She has been more attentive, but she's given no indication that she wants to stay together and work out our problems. She's not the kind of person who would just throw eighteen years of marriage away, but then again, I've already done that for her.

Now I need to find out what's in her mind and in her heart. Especially after our visit to her parents' house. The fact that she even agreed to have Christmas Eve with them is so out of character for her, I'm still not sure what to make of it. Why did she agree to see them again after the way they've treated her? Why would she suddenly want to see them again? What was the secret conversation with her mom about? What were those three envelopes she had in her purse when we left?

Am I paranoid for thinking they were plotting against me?

When I pull into our driveway, Kyle is still hounding Grace for his Christmas presents, and she's still pretending she didn't get him anything.

"Come on, Mom. You know you don't want to wait until tomorrow. You can give it to me now and sleep late in the morning."

We walk in, and Kyle heads straight for the den. I get the fireplace going while Grace disappears upstairs, most likely to get his gift.

"Dad, can we give Mom her gifts tonight?"

"You can give her the one from you. I want to give her mine when we're alone."

"Cool."

After the fire is roaring again, Grace joins us, carrying two large boxes. I rush to take them out of her arms. The boxes are long and wide—and heavy.

"Babe, why didn't you tell me? I would've carried these down for you."

Her eyes meet mine, and the sadness in them is like a punch to my stomach. I haven't called her "babe" in forever, but it just flowed effortlessly from my tongue. As if nothing had ever changed between us.

"It's okay. I managed to carry them upstairs and wrap them when I bought them. I'm stronger than you think."

"I know you are," I say sincerely.

When I put both boxes in front of Kyle, Grace smiles and takes one away. His face drops, and he looks disappointed. Grace laughs and shakes her head. "Cut it out, you big baby."

Kyle's grin breaks free, and he throws his head back in laughter. "That look never has worked on you."

"Not when you're faking it. I can tell when you're really sad and when you're trying to pull a fast one."

She looks at me and inclines her head toward the couch. "Sit down so you can open yours."

"Mine? But I thought the patio and fire pit were my gifts."

"They are, but this is just a little something extra."

I do as she asks because I'm too confused to argue. The presents have been in her bedroom for a while, since before I started working from home. That means she got them before she confronted me about Tammy.

Why would she do that?

She puts the box in my lap and steps back to watch both of us open them. Kyle's vigorous tearing of wrapping paper catches my attention, and I can't help but smile at how thrilled he is. The boy is as big as me, and he's still like a little kid when it comes to Christmas.

"Mom, you are the best!" He jumps up with the still half-wrapped package under one arm and loops his free arm around her. "Thank you."

They turn to me, his arm still draped over her shoulders, and wait for me to unwrap mine. So I tear off the paper and stare incredulously at the picture on the box.

"My God. I haven't done this in years. Are you two plotting to kill me?" I laugh and open the box.

"Are you kidding, Dad? This is a top-of-the-line snowboard. We are gonna own those slopes!"

Grace kneels and pulls a small, flat box from under the tree. "Here you go."

Kyle opens it without a moment's hesitation, pulls out an envelope, and begins to pump his fist in the air. "Yes! Yes!" He grabs Grace again and kisses her on the cheek. "I love you, Mom."

He hands the envelope to me, and inside, I find a certificate for reservations at the premiere snowboarding slopes in northern Vermont. In one week. In a two-bedroom suite.

"It says the reservations are for four. Are you coming with us?" I ask Grace.

"No, I can't. That's my long weekend at work. I'm covering for a friend one day. So, I thought you two could go and take Wes and Alan with you."

"Perfect! Dad, can we do that?"

"Sure," I reply to Kyle but keep my eyes trained on Grace. She fidgets under my scrutiny. She's hiding something.

"Okay, have a seat, Mom. I want you to open your gift."

Kyle wrapped the small earring box inside several other boxes, each bigger than the previous. He finally stopped when he reached a box big enough to hold a window air conditioning unit. Weeding through all the boxes and paper takes Grace a while to find her actual gift.

When she finally opens the small velvet box, she is shocked speechless. One hand covers her open mouth, and tears spring to her eyes. She swallows back a sob as she continues to stare at them.

"Kyle...Blake...you shouldn't have."

"Are you kidding? My mom is the best, so she deserves the best. Try them on. Let's make sure we got your size," he jokes.

She takes them out, tears still shimmering in her eyes, and carefully replaces her current earrings with the diamond studs. When she looks at them in the mirror, she can no longer control her emotions. "They're gorgeous. And they fit perfectly."

She turns and hugs Kyle, thanking him for the thoughtful gift. I stand and wait for my turn, eager to have her in my arms and to feel her willing embrace against me again. She looks at me when she releases Kyle and stretches her arms toward me. I step into her space, and she wraps her arms around my neck. My hands glide around her waist until they meet, and I draw her entire body into mine.

"Mmm, Grace," I murmur into her ear. Then she melts into me a little more as her body betrays her attempt at self-preservation. She tries to hide how much she's affected by me, how badly she still wants me, until we touch. Then she can't hide what she really wants and needs any more than I can.

"Thank you for these. They're gorgeous."

"You are gorgeous, Grace. These diamonds can't hold a candle to you."

"Still such a sweet talker." She releases me and wipes the tears from her eyes. "I still can't believe you got me diamond earrings."

"You've always wanted them. We figured it was about time you got them," Kyle replies.

"I wish I'd gotten them for you years ago. But I'll focus on spoiling you so much more in the future."

She quickly hides the sadness in her eyes. But not quickly enough to hide it from me.

Satisfied with opening his big gift, Kyle leaves Grace and me alone on the couch. The fire and the twinkling tree are our only light. My back is against the armrest, and her back is against my chest. My arms are around her, and I realize we feel so right together.

"I love my earrings. Thank you." Her voice is soft with a hint of sleep.

Maybe if I keep holding her, keeping her warm, she'll fall asleep in my arms tonight.

"Kyle picked them out. Getting those for you was very important to him."

"He's the best kid. I don't know what I'll do without him when he leaves."

That reminder makes me flinch involuntarily. My muscles tense, and my heart skips a beat before it starts jackhammering against my ribs. She misinterprets my reaction and tries to get up, but I lock my arms around her.

"I don't want you to go. Stay with me tonight."

"Blake, why even pretend now? You're gone as soon as Kyle is gone. We both know this act won't last much longer. You got caught up in pretending nothing has happened and fooled yourself into thinking you were happy with me again. But the minute reality hits home, as soon as Kyle's gone, you'll be gone too."

"Yes, I messed up. I got lost, but I'm not pretending about anything now. This isn't an elaborate act I'm all caught up in, Grace. But I am trying to give you time and space to work this out in your mind. This is the marriage I want—that I've always wanted. This is the bond I want us to have. This is the couple I want us to be—sharing everything, doing everyday things together, spending time together every chance we get. You have to see my intentions are true and feel my love for you is real before you'll believe my words. Let me show you, babe. Stay here in my arms tonight. Just let me hold you."

She relaxes against me but doesn't respond. She doesn't need to, though. I already know what I need to know.

She isn't ready to accept the rings I bought her yet.

CHAPTER 8

Grace

"*B*lake's confession Christmas Eve threw me for a loop. I know he said something similar after our shopping excursion, but I didn't put much stock in it because I thought he was just caught up in the charade. When he said this is how he has always wanted us to be, it just felt different. I ended up falling asleep in his arms and slept better than I have in ages," I tell Leigh over coffee.

"How was Christmas Day?"

"Great. Kyle opened his new clothes while Blake and I watched. Blake's parents came over and we exchanged gifts. Then we ate all day until we were too stuffed to move. Blake convinced me to sleep on the couch with him again that night."

"Don't you think it's time to move back to your bed —together?"

"No. I'm not ready for that. It's hard enough not picturing him with her as it is. That would only make it worse."

Leigh sighs and shakes her head at me. "Grace, I love you. But you are the most stubborn person I've ever met. He's trying to make it up to you. Either let him—or let him go. You're only punishing yourself by living in limbo."

Maybe she has a point.

"He's taking me out tomorrow for New Year's Eve. He asked me on an official date. Then on New Year's Day, he and Kyle are leaving for their snowboarding trip."

"New Year's Eve, huh? That sounds like a good time to wipe the slate clean. Start over with a fresh new year. Give him the chance he's been working for over the last few weeks."

"Maybe."

"You still haven't told him everything. Have you?"

"Break is over. We need to get back to work."

While I make my rounds in the unit, Leigh's words return to me time and again. Can we begin again? Can we wipe away the past and move forward? Can I forgive him? These questions pop up again and again after I think I've already answered them. When I'm with him, I want to be with him. I want to work through the wrongs and get back to the rights. When I'm away from him, the doubts creep back in and nearly suffocate me.

That damn letter in my pantry also changes everything. Just when I think maybe we can have a future, the words on that innocuous looking paper mock me, stealing any happiness I think I've found. A new patient in the ICU takes my full attention, and I'm more than willing to spend the next couple of hours focused on his medical history and the doctor's orders for his care. Concentrating on something else gives me a reprieve from my chaotic life.

By the time I head home, I'm physically and mentally exhausted. When I walk in, the house smells delicious—lasagna, garlic bread, and tiramisu are waiting for me somewhere. I'd know those scents anywhere. I follow my nose to the kitchen and find my husband at the stove. He has a hand towel draped over his shoulder as he mixes a salad with tongs.

Candles sit in the middle of the table that's already set with plates, napkins, silverware, and the food. He looks over at me and smiles. He's so handsome—even more so now than when we were love-struck teenagers. Years and experience have given him a more refined appearance. Age has given him fuller features. While I thought he was muscular when we were young, he's bulked up even more as a man. His black hair has a few sprinkles of gray, giving him a sexy pepper with a little bit of salt look.

"I hope you're hungry. I made enough food to feed a small army."

"I'm starving, and it all smells delicious. Can I help with anything?"

"No, babe, I have it all under control. Have a seat. I'll open the wine, and we can eat."

My heart melts and hurts at the same time. He's enjoying spoiling me, and I'm enjoying being spoiled by him. For now, I decide to thoroughly enjoy my night and my time with my husband. Worry and stress haven't resulted in anything good, so maybe just going with the flow will.

Dinner is absolutely delicious, and the company is as well. We laugh, we talk, we reminisce, and every second of it is perfect—even when it's awkward, even when it's uncomfortable, even when it feels like so much has changed between us. It's perfect because it's real.

When we finish eating and drinking all the wine, we move to the sink and clean the dishes together. Working side by side, we have the kitchen spotless in no time. Kyle is out with his girlfriend, so Blake and I have the house to ourselves.

And I have butterflies in my chest...and in my stomach...and in other unexpected places.

Blake takes my hand in his and leads me to the couch. He sits, pulls me down beside him, and wraps his arm around me. I snuggle into him, craving the contact and safety of his embrace, and he grabs the remote to turn on the TV.

"Relax, Grace. I'm not pushing you for anything. I just want to spend time with you. I don't even care what we do—watching TV or going out on the town doesn't make a difference. As long as we're together."

I want to believe him. So badly.

"Blake! Get out here right now!" A female voice screams from outside, in my front yard. A young female voice. Blake freezes— his whole body goes rigid at once. He's as shocked as I am. He doesn't move a muscle as he stares at the front door.

"You've got to be shitting me." He finally stands and strides to the door then stops and turns to me. "I'm so sorry, Grace. For this —her showing up here. For everything. I'm such a fucking idiot."

He jerks the door open and steps onto the front porch. I fly up off the couch and stomp up behind him. She's at my home—her ass is mine.

"Tammy, what the fuck are you doing here?" Blake demands.

She staggers, barely in control of her faculties. Obviously drunk. Her crookedly parked car, half over the curb into my yard, is more proof she's in no shape to be out driving. She's standing on my front lawn making a fool of herself while my neighbors watch, peeking out their windows.

"I'm here because *she* is trying to take you away from me. I love you, Blake. Leave her. I miss you so much," she begs loudly while slurring her words. "That old bitch doesn't love you or appreciate you. I do. I'm the one you love and the one you want."

"No, actually, you're not. I love my wife, Tammy. I've always loved her, and I will love her until the day I die. I asked you to stay away, but you came here and disrespected my family. You will leave here and never come back. If you do, I'll have to call the police and report you. I'll call you a cab and a tow truck this time —you're not driving away from here drunk like this. But this is the only time I'll do this. Next time, I'll let the police handle you." Blake turns to grab his phone from inside, and Tammy turns her anger toward me.

"You! You did this. You and your demands on him. He doesn't

love you—he loves me. Why don't you just let him go and save some of your dignity? You're pathetic."

"That's funny. I'm not the one who's drunk, standing in the yard of a married man's house, begging him to leave his wife. From where I stand, you're the pathetic one. I'm the one he comes home to, the one he holds at night when he sleeps, the one he vowed to spend his life with. I'm his wife. You're no one to him."

The verbal slap my words delivers stings her exactly as I intended. She's stunned speechless for a few seconds. Then she screams like a banshee and charges toward me. Her hands are curled into fists, and I have no doubt she intends to take our exchange to the next level. That's fine with me, though, since I'd like nothing better myself.

When she gets close enough, she rears her fist back and prepares to punch me, but I stop her cold with a hard jab to her nose. I feel her flesh give way under my knuckles and hear the crunch of bone as it breaks. She flies backward, landing in the grass on her back. Blood streams out of her nose and smears across her cheek. Then the cold night air is once again filled with her shrieks.

"You broke my fucking nose! You bitch! I'll kill you!" Her words are garbled from the instant swelling and her hand covering most of her face.

"You stay the fuck away from her!" Blake yells, stepping in front of me. "So help me God, Tammy."

Flashing lights and sirens fill the street on my block. My next-door neighbor steps outside and points her finger at Tammy. "It was her, officers. She attacked my neighbor. Drove over here drunk and was yelling like a crazy woman. Woke up half the neighborhood."

The police take our statements and perform a sobriety test on Tammy. After she blows into the Breathalyzer, the officer puts the handcuffs on her and arrests her—in my front yard. Her car that

Blake offered to have towed is now being impounded, and she's facing multiple charges.

Blake watches the entire scene unfold with a detached expression on his face, but I feel the anger building just beneath his surface. When the free circus show is over, we retreat to the privacy of our home, but his pent-up frustration won't let him relax. He paces back and forth across the length of our living room, running his fingers through his hair and ranting to himself.

I sit on the couch and smile to myself, reliving the very second when I punched her in the face as hard as I could. That moment couldn't have been more perfect.

"Why are you smiling?" Blake stops mid-stride and stares at me as if I've lost my mind.

"Because I got to break her nose," I reply. "And she got arrested, and they impounded her car. All in all, it has been a good night."

Blake is silent while he contemplates my words, then throws his head back in laughter. "You never cease to amaze me. Here I am, convinced she just ruined any chance I have of getting you back, and you're enjoying yourself. If it'll help you forgive me and love me again, I'll let you break my nose. Hell, you can break my kneecaps if that's what it takes."

He kneels in front of me and wedges himself between my legs. His hands cup my face. "I'm so sorry, babe. I'm sorry for giving up on us. I'm sorry for not being the husband and father I should've been. I'm sorry for hurting you and our marriage. I wish I could take back every second of it."

I lift my hand to place it on his cheek but wince in pain when I move my fingers. He looks down at my swollen knuckles with concern in his eyes. "Shit, babe. Look what you did to your hand. Do we need to go get it X-rayed?"

"Nah." I shake my head. "I'll just ice it, and it'll be fine tomorrow."

He goes to the kitchen and comes back with a bag of ice and

gently places it on my swollen hand. Then he resumes his place wedged between my knees. "What else can I do to make us right again? Name it, and I'll do it."

"We just have to give ourselves time, Blake. That's all we can do."

He leans in and kisses my lips. I'm overtly aware of everything I feel at this second. Earlier today, I thought his intimate touch would repulse me. But the feel of his full lips against mine makes my senses detonate like pyrotechnics. His tongue caresses the part in my lips, and I yield to him, giving him full access. His arms wrap around me and pull me toward him. Our bodies are crushed together, his mouth devours mine, and his tongue caresses mine with each stroke. My body temperature rises. With every passing second, my resolve to keep my distance from him wanes.

My legs wrap around his waist, and I hold him even closer to me. The friction of our movements sends bolts of electricity through my every nerve. I didn't think I would—or could—want him again. But I do. Every cell inside me screams for the pleasure only he can give. For the one man who has always owned my heart. Even when he broke it, he still owned all the shattered pieces.

The sound of a car door slamming shut pulls us from our impromptu make-out session. Blake pulls back and stares deep into my eyes, his love for me swimming in the dark pools of his chocolate-brown eyes. "Kyle is staying at Alan's house tomorrow night while we're out on our date. Maybe we can pick this back up then. If not, it'll still be the best night of my life, because I'll be with you."

Before I can reply, Kyle walks through the door from the garage into the kitchen. Blake takes his seat on the couch beside me, and we cuddle together while watching a movie. But my mind is not on the TV at all. We chat with Kyle for a few minutes before he retreats to his room. Then Blake and I resume our new ritual of changing into our pajamas and falling asleep together on the couch. Before I drift off to sleep, I picture us spooning in our bed tomorrow night.

~

It's New Year's Eve, and I'm in my bedroom getting ready for my date tonight. I can't shake the nervous energy that has settled in my stomach. I feel like I'm going on my first date. Blake has kept the plans a complete secret—he only said to dress up and wear my sexy heels. With my makeup on lock, my hair styled, and my shimmery little black dress on, I slide my feet into my strappy heels and head downstairs to find Blake.

He's waiting in the den and stands when he hears my heels click across the hardwood floor. His eyes fly wide open, and his jaw drops. Maybe I haven't paid enough attention to my appearance lately. Maybe if I'd seen this kind of reaction from him more often, I wouldn't have become so complacent in our relationship.

"Wow. You are so beautiful you take my breath away." The hunger in his eyes is palpable. He circles me like a predator cornering its prey. "I don't deserve you, I fully admit that. But I will be a man you'll be proud to call your husband. I will show you that one enormous mistake doesn't define me. If you'll stay with me, you will never regret it."

He senses that I can't answer that lingering question just yet and gives a single nod of understanding. He slips my coat off the rack and wraps it around my shoulders from behind me. "Grace, I thought my mind was playing tricks on me last night, but now I'm sure of it. You've lost weight. Are you okay?"

"Yes, I'm okay. I don't think I've lost that much."

He presses his forehead against the back of my head. "This is all my fault. I've caused you so much stress and pain. I can't tell you how much I regret every second of the time I was with her. I'll tell you I'm sorry every day for the rest of our lives."

I turn to face him with Leigh's advice in the forefront of my mind. "Blake, I don't want that—not for you and not for me. The best thing we can do now is move forward one step and one day at a time. We can't do that constantly looking behind us. I just can't commit fully yet—it was only a few weeks ago that you were sure you wanted someone else. I haven't had enough time to recover from that. We've both made mistakes and taken each other for granted, but I do believe you regret what happened."

He pulls me into his arms and holds me tight against him. "I understand, babe. We'll start over—dating, getting to know each other again, spending time together. And soon, you'll see how much I love you and don't want to lose you. And you'll remember how much you love me, too."

He helps me into my coat, and we walk out to the car. "You never told me where we're going."

"I know." He waggles his eyebrows. "It's a surprise."

Our small Vermont town doesn't have a lot of places that could hold a surprise, so I have a feeling we're headed out of town for the night. He heads north toward the mountains, and I look over at him, confused. "Aren't you and Kyle headed this way in the morning?"

"Yeah, but we have plenty of time tonight. I don't mind no sleep tonight if you don't mind sleeping in the car on the way home."

"I don't mind at all."

He reaches over and takes my hand in his. "I should've asked first. I keep forgetting you're going in on your day off tomorrow. Maybe I should reschedule our plans tonight so you can rest. You've been too stressed as it is."

"No, don't you dare. I've been looking forward to tonight. I've worked on fewer hours of sleep than I'll get tonight. I'll rest when I get off work tomorrow night. You and Kyle will be away, and I won't have anything else to do."

"If you're sure..." He doesn't sound convinced.

"I'm positive."

We arrive about thirty minutes later, and I'm in complete awe. I never knew this place existed, and I wonder how many years we've missed out on experiencing the magic. We're at the North Pole—recreated—in this small mountain town. A huge, beautiful tree sits in the middle of the town square that's cordoned off from traffic. The roads leading into town have been cleared, but the streets comprising the square haven't, so the snow is much deeper, giving the city a surreal feeling.

Elves dart back and forth from a small house to the center of the square, leaving wrapped presents under the tree, but with "Happy New Year" wrapping paper instead of Christmas. A horse-drawn sleigh stops near the tree, letting people on and off before making another pass around the town center. A train whistle blows, drawing my eyes to the huge steam locomotive that's every bit as festive as the rest of the town.

"Blake, this place is perfect. I love it."

"Want to walk around and window-shop before we board the train?" He produces two North Pole All-Access Pass train tickets with a shy smile. "I thought about the traditional New Year's Eve parties—dancing, drinking, elbowing through hordes of people. But I decided against that. I'd rather have a night focused on you."

"I'd love to walk around for a bit. I can't promise to only window-shop, though. There may be something here I can't live without."

He gets out and rushes around to open my door and help me out of the car. All this attention is addictive—but I think that's part of his plan. To make me realize he's the only thing I can't live without. We walk hand in hand down the covered sidewalk, admiring the window scenes and festive decorations.

An elderly man steps out of one of the shops and smiles warmly at us. "Would you like some hot apple cider to warm you?"

"Sure, sounds delicious." We walk in his shop behind him, and I'm immediately glad we did. The old, nostalgic shop has so many unique items, I can't stop myself from walking around the store to admire everything. There are so many hidden treasures in here, we may end up taking the whole store home.

Then one simple display catches my eye while the shop owner and Blake chat. I walk to it and take it all in. The cover of the book on display reads: *"How to Heal Your Marriage."* I take the book out of the clear package and open it to the first page. The advice, displayed in huge font, is: **You will begin to heal when you let go of past hurts.**

I turn the page and find a list of numbers with blank lines beside each one. At the top of the page, the instructions read: **Make a list of all the ways your spouse has hurt you. Think hard, go through every memory, and don't leave anything out.**

My eyes scroll down the numbers, mentally ticking off each hurt, regret, and angry moment that comes to mind. When I reach the bottom of the page, I inhale sharply and grip the book tighter.

Now, tear this page out, throw it away, and never return to these memories again.

Blake moves up beside me with a cup of apple cider. "Did you find something you want?"

"No." I shake my head. "But I did find a bunch of things I want to throw away, though."

His brows draw down, and he tilts his head, questioning my meaning. I take the cup from his hand and offer him the book. He reads the first two pages, and understanding lights in his eyes.

"You're sure? You're ready?"

"I'm still scared. But we're not promised to tomorrow, and we've let too many yesterdays pass us by. Today is all we have."

"You won't regret it. I promise, Grace."

The train whistle blows again, alerting us it's time to go. We thank the man for the drinks and rush to the platform. The decorations in the main car are amazing. I feel like we stepped into a world of glamour and glitz. They spared no expense in preparing the train to ring in the new year.

We move to the next car, and the smell of food immediately hits us. After filling our plates with finger foods and grabbing a flute of champagne each, we continue our exploration of the remaining cars. The last one we can enter is the one I want to spend the entire ride inside. The top is clear, giving us an unobstructed view of the night sky and falling snow. It's beautiful and magical.

We stay in the car alone until the train reaches full speed, then Blake convinces me to rejoin the party car. The music is fast and loud when we enter. The beat thumps in my ears and chest until my feet refuse to remain still. We begin dancing, moving closer and closer, until we're grinding on each other in a heated rhythm. Everyone around us disappears, and only Blake and I exist.

The song turns slow and melodic. Bodies join two by two, and the car darkens. The overhead string lights sparkle like starlight shimmering in the black sky. I wrap my arms around his neck, his go around my waist, and we meld together, moving as one. His lips find my neck and leave a trail of white-hot kisses from the hollow of my shoulder to the lobe of my ear. Shivers race up and down my spine, extending out to my arm as goose bumps.

Putty. I'm putty in this man's hands.

I love the train. I love the thought he put into this surprise. I love how we've overcome obstacles and made each other a priority again.

But right now, I wish we were home alone.

His mouth finds mine, and he claims it, staking his territory with every caress of his tongue. The slow burn ignites into a raging inferno, consuming us both to the point we nearly lose all self-control on the dance floor. When the song ends, we break our kiss, but our faces remain a breath apart.

Midnight feels like a lifetime away.

CHAPTER 9

Blake

Grace is asleep beside me while I drive home from our first date in...I couldn't even say how long. Every plan I made for tonight was to remind her of how great we were together at one time and to show her we can be again. I'd say my plan worked by the peaceful expression on her face. She must be tired after a long night of shopping, dinner, dancing, and making out.

That last part plays on a continuous loop in my mind. I want nothing more than to pull over, wake her, and finish what we started on the train. But I won't do that. She has to get up early to get to the hospital on time then work a long twelve hours. Plus, she has an extra day of work this weekend, so she needs all the rest she can get.

I've already decided to give her all the control in our relationship. When she wants to make love to me again—*if* she ever does—it'll be on her terms, her time frame, and her call. At the time, I thought an appointment for a checkup was useless. I was leaving her and moving on with someone else. Now, I'm beyond relieved I followed through, regardless of how humiliating asking my doctor for STD testing was at the time.

Whether she believes I was never unprotected or not, at least she knows that's one less point of this mess she needs to worry about.

I reach over and place my hand on her bare leg, rubbing the supple skin of her thigh. She whimpers lightly in her sleep and slides her leg closer to me. I wonder if she even realizes she's doing it until her hand slides up my arm in an affectionate motion. Her breathing evens out again, but she keeps the constant contact with me. I choose to take this as another good sign that we're moving in the right direction.

When we get home, I wrap her coat around her before I lift her from the seat and carry her in my arms. She curls into my chest, barely waking when I move her. With my lips pressed against her temple, I pull her body against mine. I hate to do it, but I have to wake her to unlock the door.

"Grace, sweetheart," I say softly.

"Hmm," she objects, and I chuckle.

"I have to put you down for a minute to unlock the door, babe."

She opens her sleepy eyes and prepares to stand while I finagle the doorknob. Once it's open, she walks clumsily inside with a mixture of alcohol and fatigue bungling her steps. I wrap my arm around her, acting as her crutch, and she leans into me again. I kiss the top of her head, just to release the strong feelings inside me that threaten to overflow.

She remains guarded with me. I still feel the distance between us. She's keeping me at arm's length even after she said she wanted to put the past behind us. Maybe I'm chasing her, begging for her love and affection once again, but I'm okay with that for now. My egregious mistake was my own, but I've realized at last what I wanted and needed was the love of my life back. I won't stop until I have all of her again—heart, body, and mind.

"Are you sleeping with me tonight?" I ask.

"Yes. I'll change for bed and be right back down." She raises up on her toes and kisses me, her sweet lips pressed against mine, and I lift her into my arms again.

"Let me help you."

Inside our bedroom upstairs, I put her down and undress her. She watches me with hooded eyes and ragged breaths. I use every bit of self-control and willpower in my arsenal when I pull her long T-shirt over her head and point her toward the bathroom. While she washes her face and brushes her teeth, I stare longingly at the bed we used to share. She's not prepared to take that step this early, I get it. I haven't slept in it with her for a long time now.

When she finishes, I make quick work of my bedtime routine and find her asleep at the foot of the bed.

Waiting for me.

After I have us settled on the couch, she snuggles against me, and I slip into a deep sleep. So deep, I don't feel her get up for work or hear her moving around the house while she dresses. I don't even hear her open and close the door when she leaves. When I wake up, I find a note in her vacant spot telling me and Kyle to enjoy our trip and take lots of pictures. She says she wants to hear all about it when we get home.

While I love her thoughtfulness, her sentiments serve to remind me we'll spend a weekend apart just when we're beginning to grow closer. I only hope this all-guys' trip doesn't backfire on me in the form of a setback in the progress we've made. Insecurity rears its ugly head and makes me question if she'll realize she's happier without me here...if what I've done is too much to overcome...that she doesn't love me anymore.

I didn't tell her the news I received from work today when I checked my email for any urgent matters. An announcement was sent out alerting the team of Tammy's departure from our office. Since I have insider knowledge, I know she lost her job because of her arrest in my front yard. Driving under the influence of drugs or alcohol isn't tolerated by the company for any reason.

Technically, I can return to the corporate office now to work since Tammy isn't there, but I don't want to. After working from home the past month and spending so much time with Grace during her off days, I don't want to give that up. Even just stealing a few minutes between my conference calls and in-person meetings has made a world of difference in me, in her, and in our relationship. I can sense her apprehension of giving me another chance, but I can also tell she wants our marriage to work as much as I do.

It gives me hope.

Before I lived through this nightmare myself, I believed the adage "once a cheater, always a cheater." But now, I don't believe those words at all. I've learned my lesson in the worst possible manner, but I am man enough to admit my faults. The thought of losing her cripples me. The possibility of never feeling her love again crushes me. But the opportunity we have to strengthen and make our relationship better than before empowers me.

I'm no longer lost. I'm no longer wandering, looking for what I thought was missing in my life. I'm home, and I've realized how vital that connection is. I'm right where I'm meant to be, where I was always meant to be.

Kyle, Wes, and Alan walk in as I'm enjoying the last cup of coffee. "Look what the cat dragged in. I'm surprised I didn't have to threaten you three to get out of bed this morning."

"No way, Mr. Hardy. We've been so excited to go we hardly slept at all last night. We're packed and ready to leave whenever you are," Alan replies.

"We can even leave right this minute because we've already put our stuff in the car. That's how ready we are," Kyle adds. "And we noticed your bag is already in the car too."

"And if you decide we need to stay an extra night, we can arrange to make that happen too," Wes chimes in.

"All right, boys. I get the hint." I turn and rinse my coffee cup, and my thoughts immediately return to Grace. She's in everything I do. "Let's hit the road."

A weekend away with three hormonal teenage boys. Now I wonder if this was a thoughtful gift from my wife, or a really sneaky revenge plot that also gives her a great laugh at my expense. Either way, Kyle's excitement can't be contained, so we're off to the alpines to snowboard for a couple of days. The boys whoop and holler all the way to the car, and I decide I can put away my responsible hat for the weekend and be one of the guys. Mostly.

After we're settled into the suite Grace so kindly reserved for us, Kyle and his gang of juvenile miscreants won't even give me time to call and let her know we've arrived safely. Before we leave the room, I send her a quick text with a promise to call her later tonight. Knowing these boys, we'll be out on the slopes all day and crawling back to the room well after dark without an ounce of energy left.

When we reach the top of the chairlift, none of us can contain our eagerness. The sun is bright, and the powder is perfect. One run after another, we glide downhill, switching up the trails from challenging to easy and fun, then back again. Through the wipe-outs and the Olympic-worthy runs, Kyle and I reconnect in a way we never have before. Not as father and son, but as friends with a bond that's unbreakable.

This day never would've happened without Grace. The immense gratitude I feel toward her leaves me speechless. She didn't have to do any of this—giving me another chance, pushing me to be the father our son deserves, making me want to be the husband I always should've been. Through every good day and bad day and mistake and stroke of luck, she has been my saving grace. Even when I was too stupid to realize it. Even when I didn't deserve her.

After spending a full day on the slopes and half the evening at the restaurant, we finally make it back to the room. The boys head for the second bedroom to play video games while I crash in the master bedroom, ready to talk to my wife. Alone. I close the bedroom door and settle onto the bed. I call her cell phone.

No answer.

I try FaceTime.

No answer.

I call the house phone, glad she never listened to me when I insisted we needed to cancel the landline to save money.

No answer.

I scrape my hand down my face as I sit up, throwing my legs over the side of the bed. Part of me wants to drive straight home and check on her. It's not like her to let calls go unanswered, especially knowing we've been on the slopes and someone could've been hurt. For a moment, I briefly consider calling our next-door neighbor and having her check on Grace for me, just in case something is wrong. Then I glance at the time and realize she's probably already asleep after working a long day then going back early tomorrow morning to do it all over again.

Day two on the slopes is pretty much a repeat of day one—all the fun, making our relationship even more sound, and being goofy with the guys. But I do take a midday break to rest my tired muscles, unwilling to admit I find it harder to keep up with the young whippersnappers than I thought it would be. Not talking to Grace for two days is messing with my head, so I call the hospital on the off chance she's due for a break.

"ICU. How can I help you?" the nurse answers.

"Hi, is there any way I can I speak to Grace Hardy?"

"Grace? I don't see her in the unit right now."

"Okay, thanks. I'll just try her at home later."

I'm disappointed but not surprised. Grace never takes her cell phone into the unit with her. She says she's too busy to check it anyway, and we know to call the direct unit number in the event of an emergency. If I could get away with claiming this is an emergency, I would do it in a heartbeat. But since her coworker doesn't see her in the unit, that means she's probably in one of the rooms with a patient, and she'd be pissed if I interrupted her when there wasn't a real emergency.

Later at dinner, Kyle surprises me.

"Have you talked to Mom? I haven't heard from her at all. That's not like her—I usually have at least a text from her telling me she loves me and to be careful."

I tamp down the panic rising in my chest. Grace hasn't even contacted Kyle. That's completely out of character for her.

"No, I haven't. I tried to call a couple of times, but she hasn't answered.

He tries to disguise it, but I know Kyle is worried. "I sent her a text before we ordered, and she still hasn't answered me. She could be just really busy at work and tired when she gets home. I don't know. Maybe we should head back in the morning, just in case."

My seventeen-year-old son proposing to give up an entire day on the slopes to go home early and check on his mom fills me with trepidation. Like a bad omen or a black cloud hanging over us, we both feel something is off. Something is wrong.

When she doesn't answer my calls at eight o'clock, then nine o'clock, then ten o'clock, I march into the boys' game cave and tell them to pack. I can't wait any longer to get home and check on my wife. Wes and Alan pile into the back seat, and Kyle sits in the front with me.

"You're worried," he says.

"I am." I glance over my shoulder at him. "So are you."

He nods. "Yep. We talk every day. She's always made it a point to make me tell her about my day, no matter how shitty hers was. She always wants to know all about it."

"She loves you." I can't even tell him I never realized she had that ritual with him. She found a way to connect with him during a time when most kids his age start to pull away from their parents. She and I should've been doing that together all along. Our little family would've been so much stronger had I had my head screwed on straight.

"She loves you too, Dad."

I hope my son is correct. I hope my wife still loves me.

It's after two o'clock in the morning by the time we get back into our sleepy little neighborhood and drop Wes and Alan off at their houses. I'm in such a hurry, I tell them they can get their bags tomorrow. I have to get home to her. Now.

When I turn into the driveway, the first thing I notice is her car is in the driveway. All the lights in the house are off—even the light in the den we usually leave on all the time. Kyle and I rush to the door and find the inside of the house is eerily quiet. Too quiet for my comfort level. She's not on the couch, so I bound up the stairs and rush into the bedroom.

The room is pitch-black with the curtains drawn, so I flip on the light switch. The covers on the bed are crumpled and messy, and one side is bunched up more than the other, not the way she normally leaves it. I stomp across the room, panic settled in my chest. Her car is here, but she's not.

Is she off somewhere with another man?

Insane jealousy overtakes my rational mind and visions of her in another man's arms, in his bed, doing the things that only I should do with her take up residence in my thoughts. When I turn on my heel, stalking back toward the door to hunt the mother-fucker down and relieve him of his swinging dick, I stop dead in my tracks.

Those aren't bunched-up covers…that's Grace, covered from head to toe under the comforter and completely oblivious to our presence. Even with the overhead light on.

I rush to the side of the bed and gently shake her shoulder. Kyle hurries over, as surprised as I am that she's been here this whole time, and calls her name. She barely stirs.

"Grace, talk to me, or I'm calling an ambulance," I order. Fear and panic claw at me, but I hold those feelings at bay until I can calm down and assess the situation.

She fights to open her eyes for a split second, then they clamp shut again. "Blake?" she asks, her voice groggy and thick with sleep.

"Yeah, babe. We're home. What's wrong with you? Are you sick?" I push the comforter off her head to let the light in and hopefully wake her up more.

"I'm okay. Just really tired." Her words are slightly slurred. Has she been drinking? Who has she been out with? And where?

"Mom, I'm worried about you. Do we need to take you to the ER?"

She shakes her head. "No, baby. I'll be okay. I just need to sleep."

Kyle cuts his eyes up to me with a dubious expression covering his face. "I'll stay in here with her and make sure she's okay. You go get some rest yourself, and we'll see how she feels in the morning."

"Okay. Wake me if anything changes."

Kyle leaves us alone, and I crawl onto the bed behind Grace but lie on top of the covers because I'm still not sure she wants me in here, in our bed. Shoving aside thoughts of jealousy and fear of her possible infidelity, I wrap my arms around her so I can feel her breathe because my concern for her well-being overrides my mistrust. But I don't get a single wink of sleep the rest of the night.

I have so many unanswered questions.

So many suspicions.

So many doubts.

And a broken heart with a hefty dose of poetic justice.

CHAPTER 10

Grace

When my alarm goes off, I barely have enough energy to move. I reach over and slap the clock just to stop the irritating noise. If I close my eyes again, I know I'll be out like a light and will most likely miss the snooze alarm. Sitting up takes too much effort, so I roll off the side of the bed, letting my feet hit the floor a half second before it's too late to catch myself. I stumble into the bathroom and get the hot water flowing. By the time I get out, I feel a little better than before, but not much.

I don't know how much longer I can keep this up.

Dressed and ready for work, I walk out of my bedroom and come to a complete stop when I reach the top of the stairs. The bright light from the kitchen illuminates the steps and the foyer, and I know I didn't leave it on last night. In fact, I didn't go into the kitchen at all after I got home.

I creep down the stairs, careful not to make a sound, preparing myself to peek around the corner. My heart is pounding against the inside of my chest so hard I wouldn't be surprised if the intruder hears it before he hears me. And what am I going to do if he's still in here? I grab my phone from my pocket and dial 9-1-1 —then wait to hit send. When I glance into the kitchen, my hand falls to my side as my mouth drops open.

"Blake?" He's leaning against the counter with his arms folded over his chest.

"Morning," he replies casually. Maybe a little aloof.

I look around the room, trying to get my bearings. I feel so lost.

"It's Sunday morning, right? I didn't sleep through the whole day, did I?"

His head tilts to the side ever so slightly while he studies me with narrowed eyes. "Yes, it's still Sunday morning. Very early Sunday morning, as a matter of fact. I see you're dressed for work."

"Of course I'm dressed for work. What else would I be dressed for at this time of the morning? What are you doing home so early? Is everyone okay?"

I walk farther into the kitchen to get a bottle of water before I leave for work, and Blake pushes off the counter, blocking me from the refrigerator door. His eyes never leave mine as his hand grips the door handle. But he doesn't answer me.

"Want me to make you a cup of coffee?" he asks.

"No thank you. I just want some water. I'm very thirsty this morning."

He reaches inside, grabs the bottle, then takes my hand in his other one before pulling me toward the table. "Have a seat."

He opens the bottle and sets it in front of me. I pick it up, ready to take a drink. "Are you going to tell me what's going on?"

"Funny, I was just about to ask you that very question." He pulls away from me, his back pressed against the chair, and hardens his features.

"I'm completely lost, Blake. I have no idea what you're asking me. You're the one who's home early from a trip I bought for you and Kyle to enjoy spending time together."

"We came home because we were both worried about you, Grace. You weren't answering calls or texts. We were up in the mountains with no way to make sure you hadn't been harmed. So we rushed home late last night when you still didn't answer. You were so out of it, we talked about taking you to the emergency room. Then you said you were fine, just very tired. What the hell is going on, Grace? Are you cheating on me? Is that where you've been while I've been out of town—with him?"

The only way I'd be more surprised right now is if Blake slapped me across the face with the palm of his hand.

"You have a lot of fucking nerve to say that to me."

Suddenly, a lack of energy isn't an issue. I spring up, pushing my chair back with the force of my legs, and knock the almost full bottle of water over in the process. It spreads across the table, and Blake jumps up to grab a towel. I'd normally help clean up my own mess, but not this time. Instead, I grab my purse and coat off the rack then storm out the door toward my car.

"Grace! Grace, wait!" Blake calls from behind me, but I keep moving.

His fingers wrap around my arm, and he pulls me around to face him. His eyes search mine. A mixture of regret and sorrow swirls in the depths of his brown eyes...and fear. Whatever's on his mind, fear is at the forefront. But I stand my ground and wait for him to speak.

"Are you just going to leave me hanging like that?"

"Yes."

He runs his fingers through his hair, leaving pieces of it standing on end, and takes a step back from me. He looks disheveled but sexy. He groans in frustration, heat flashes in his eyes when he looks at me, and I once again feel the powerful undercurrent of desire that's been missing from our relationship for so long. He stalks toward me, grips my shoulders, and crushes his mouth against mine. Without asking, without waiting, he plunges his tongue into my mouth. He's taking what he wants with the most seductive force.

Only when my back bumps against my car do I realize he's walked me backward. He pushes my coat apart to run his hands over my body. Then under my shirt. Over my breasts, where his thumb lingers until my nipple peaks into a taut bud. Desire courses through me, shooting through my veins like wildfire consuming everything in its path. I wrap my arms around his neck, my fingers thread through his hair, and with every pass over my nipple, my grip tightens.

His lips move across my face, down to my neck, where a blazing hot trail of kisses leaves me gasping for air. He lifts me until my legs wrap around his waist. My scrubs and his jeans separate us, but they seem to fade away to nothing when he drives his hard cock against my core. A deep moan escapes my throat, conveying my desire much better than mere words could.

"You belong to me, Grace," he says between wet kisses against my skin. "All of you. I won't share you. I'll fight until my last breath for you."

He crushes his mouth against mine before I can reply. It occurs to me he did that on purpose. A reply isn't what he wants—he's proving his words to me one action at a time.

"Only I can fill you until it hurts so good. I'm the one who knows every inch of your body, every spot that drives you wild. I'll fucking show you who owns your body. I won't lose you when I just found you again."

Another urgent kiss is followed by the hardness of his length between my legs. My body is on fire despite the cold predawn temperature and whipping winter winds.

"Grace, touch me," he pants.

I reach between us and grasp his cock through his pants, rubbing up and down his length. His hips surge in rhythm with my hand. His hands cup my face, holding my gaze with his.

"I've missed this so much. I've missed you so much. Whatever you're doing, whoever he is, end it *now*. When you come home tonight, you're *mine* and only *mine*. And I'm yours and only yours. I swear it."

I'm stunned nearly speechless.

"Blake, are you sure you want me? In the last few months, you've been hot and cold. Loving and distant. It feels like you keep stopping yourself every time we get close, then I stop myself because I question if you'd changed your mind about us...about being attracted to me."

"Babe, I've tried to give you time to deal with everything. I've waited for you to come to me, ready for me to touch you and please you. But I'll be damned if I wait around like a whipped dog begging for forgiveness while some other man fucks my wife. If you're thinking I have no room to talk, you're absolutely right. But that won't stop me from fucking him up when I catch him.

"Listen to me, Grace. You're who I want—the only one I want. We said for better or for worse, didn't we? We've had worse. I only want better from now on. Come back to me. The thought of someone else touching you drives me fucking insane. I only want you to want me, to need me, to know I'll fulfill your needs."

The next kiss is slow and controlled but every bit as scorching hot as the frenzied, unbridled, passionate ones we started with. "When you get home tonight, we're newlyweds, retaking those vows we made. Promise me."

He squeezes me, urging me to agree to his demands. Our gaze remains locked, and we are linked by more than our physical connection. His pleas touch me deep inside, and without conscious thought or decision, I nod in agreement. When he lowers me to the ground, I realize he doesn't have a coat or shoes on, only his house slippers. He chased me out into the cold, desperate to cling to the one he loves.

Maybe I should've pursued him the same way when we started growing apart. Maybe we'd be in a much different place today.

"You won't regret it, I promise. But if he ever comes around here, I guarantee he will regret it. You've seen the pensive Blake, sorry for what he did. You've seen the sweet and romantic Blake, trying to make up for lost time. But now you're going to see the man behind it all—the one who isn't afraid to take control and take his life back. That includes taking his *wife* back."

He backs away toward the house, one slow step at a time, keeping that tether between us tight and secure. "I'll be waiting for you to get home. Be careful, babe." He pauses—both in steps and in words—and confidence exudes from his very being. "I love you, Grace."

~

WHEN I WALK through the ICU doors, Leigh is already at the nurses' station getting her briefing from the night nurse. She looks up at me, her non-poker face revealing her every emotion. The squinted eyes say she can't believe I'm here. The parted lips warn she's about to begin a very long rant. When she throws down her pen, I know she's about to throw down the gauntlet.

"What in the hell are you doing here?" she demands.

"Working," My blasé tone is accentuated by a dismissive shrug, as if the answer is obvious and she should already know it.

"Grace, come on. Even you have to admit this is a bad idea."

"We're already short-handed. Let's just make it through today, then I have four days off."

"Fine. But we're working together today. I'm helping you with your patients, and I'm not taking no for an answer."

"When do you ever?" I retort with a smile.

"Have you told him yet?" She stands and puts her hand on her hip. She already knows the answer to that question too.

"Leigh, if you don't leave me alone about it, I'm going to accidentally give you a shot of Xanax and knock your lights out today."

"Promises, promises."

I love my best friend with all my heart. There's nothing I haven't shared with her. Nothing I haven't asked her advice on to help me through a tough situation. She keeps asking me about this one—specifically, if I've told Blake about it yet.

I haven't. I can't. When I found out about Tammy, I never expected to fall in love with him again. I never thought he'd fall in love with me again. My plan revolved around Kyle and getting him off to college before the world crashed and burned around us. Not telling Blake didn't start out as a secret I intentionally withheld from him—it just didn't feel like I was his business anymore.

Funny how quickly everything can change. What didn't seem important one day suddenly becomes a life-or-death matter the next. That may be a little extreme, but it drives home the point to me nonetheless. I agreed to be his and only his when I get home tonight. He says he's mine and only mine.

Time to test those vows we made. Again.

These thoughts spin in my mind on repeat all day. True to her word, Leigh was with me with every patient, helping me and prodding me to talk to Blake as soon as possible.

"He's done everything to earn your forgiveness and deserve your love again. The boy has it bad for you. Give him some credit and trust that he's learned from his mistakes. I'm betting on him not to fuck everything up again. You should too."

Every hour on the hour, I heard some variation of that message from Leigh. At one point, I asked if I was her best friend or if he was. Though I tried to hide it, her answer rocked me.

"You and Blake are one now. You're married to him, Grace.

You love him. I wouldn't give advice that would come between that bond."

She's right, she's right. Dammit, she's right. Any hope I had of sweeping this under the rug is gone. Any plan I had of hiding it from Kyle to protect him is futile.

I have to woman up and face this beast head on. Hopefully with Blake still at my side.

CHAPTER 11

Blake

I know the minute she walks through the door, tonight is not the night to romance her. If I thought she looked tired when she left this morning, she's a walking zombie after a long day at work. The good news is she's home exactly on time, so I know she wasn't off with some other man. The bad news is I have no idea who he is or if she works with him. He could be one of the doctors making rounds at the hospital for all I know.

Wouldn't that be karma at her fucking best?

My wife cheating on me with a doctor, of all people.

She drops her purse on the floor with her coat and slumps down onto the couch. With her head leaned back, she closes her eyes and melts into the cushions. I watch her for a moment before moving to her side.

"You need to eat. I bet you didn't even take a lunch break today."

One side of her mouth lifts. "There's never much time for a lunch in ICU. We eat on the run."

"Come with me."

She opens her eyes and gives me a puzzled look. "Where are we going?"

Despite not knowing, she puts her hand in mine, and I lead her up the stairs. In our master bathroom, a hot bubble bath waits for her to slip into the water and relax. Candles are lit around the room, and a glass of wine sits on the edge of the garden tub. Her hand flies up to cover her gaping mouth as she takes in the gesture.

"Soak in the tub. Enjoy some wine. Then when you've turned into a prune and the water has turned cold, come downstairs and have dinner with me."

"Thank you, Blake. This is perfect. I won't be too long."

"Take as long as you need, babe. I'll wait for you." I mean that, in so many more ways than one.

When she comes back downstairs, I make her plate and we eat together. She finds the energy to tell me about her day, and I hang on her every word. Partly because I want to be involved in every aspect of her life, and partly because I'm listening for a recurring male name. By the time we've finished dinner, we've talked about everything and anything, and I found nothing out of the ordinary to latch on to. Part of me thinks I'm imagining things, but then I remember how she never denied my accusations.

We settle into our place on the couch, and she falls asleep in my arms, her back to my front. Thinking back over how my affair with Tammy began, I realize how much I'd pulled away from Grace beforehand. Then I compare that fact to the way Grace is drawing closer to me. She could easily head up to the bedroom and sleep alone. She could've rejected my offer for dinner. She could've ignored me. Simply knowing she's been sleeping on the couch with me settles my torment. A little. I don't get much sleep —again—but just holding her all night comforts my racing mind.

∾

WITH THE HOLIDAYS and my vacation over, we revert to our normal routines over the following couple of weeks. Work consumes most of my days and Kyle is back in school, but I make a conscious effort to spend time alone with Grace every day. Even if I only meet her for lunch at our kitchen table. I feel the changes in her day after day—she's becoming more comfortable with me, my touch, and my love for her. When she initiates the touches and kisses, I feel invincible.

"Thank you, Blake," she says out of the blue during one of our lunch dates.

"For what?" I ask before taking a bite of my sandwich.

"I want you to know I appreciate everything you're doing for our family. For me. You're a different man today than you were just a few weeks ago. I feel real hope again, and it feels good."

"Loving you is as natural as breathing, Grace. I finally get it, what my life is all about. It's *you*. You're the only one I can't live without, and you were the one I was living without. That's why I couldn't find real happiness."

Her eyes glisten with tears. A few of them escape and drop onto her cheeks. She quickly looks away when she blots her napkin against her face. Then she reaches across the table to take my hand in hers. She laces her fingers with mine and squeezes. She surprises me when she stands and moves to my side. I slide my chair back, and she takes her seat in my lap. She wraps her arms around my neck, and I wrap mine around her waist, realizing she's lost even more weight.

"Grace, babe, I'm worried about you."

She shakes her head and crushes her mouth to mine, needy and burning for more. We're alone, and thank fuck my Friday afternoon workload is light. Kyle won't be home at all today since he's staying at Wes's house tonight. Grace and I have all the time in the world to get reacquainted with each other. And I plan to thoroughly explore her luscious body and remind her why she married me in the first place.

She turns to face me, her legs straddling mine, and her kiss becomes hungrier. My cock hardens against my zipper until her every movement makes it painful. Her fingers roam through my hair while my hands skim over her skin underneath her shirt. She whimpers into my mouth and holds my face in her hands.

Fiery passion consumes us, and before I know it, we're tugging at each other's shirts before flinging them onto the floor. Her exposed skin brushes against mine, unhinging what little bit of control I have left. My hands encircle her, and I unhook her bra before sliding it off her arms. She leans into me, her breasts pressing against my chest, as I stand with her in my arms. My hands are splayed across her back, holding her body tightly against mine, and I start for the stairs.

I break our kiss only long enough to wordlessly ask for her permission. With all we've been through, I have to know she wants this as much as I do. If she has any reservations at all, she has to tell me now. The only thing I'm certain of is I know exactly who I want to spend my life with, but I need to know where her heart and mind are.

I need to know if she's with me.

She nods, answering my unspoken question before retaking my mouth with hers. When her tongue glides across mine again, I nearly stop and fuck her up against the closest wall. Had this been any other time, I wouldn't even have thought twice about it. Her back would be against the wall, and my cock would be pounding into her. But I don't want our first time together after reconciling to be hurried or rushed. I can't fucking wait to be inside her as it is. If I stop now, we'll never make it to the bed where I can take my time driving her crazy.

I top the stairs with her still attached to me as if she weighs nothing, then we reach the bed. As I slide her pants and under-wear down her legs, I leave a trail of hot, wet kisses and watch her skin pebble with goose bumps. She's as ready as I am for this, and knowing that spurs me on even more. She sits up and unbuttons my pants before pushing them down my legs. She scoots to the edge of the bed, slides her hands in my boxer briefs, and slowly peels them off. Intentionally slow. Torturously slow.

Then she licks her lips.

Fuck me...I'm done. She has me right where she wants me. And she's right where I want her. She licks around the head of my cock, spreading the bead of moisture with her tongue. My fingers thread through her hair, and my head drops back between my shoulder blades. When she takes me in deep, I feel the back of her throat against the tip of my dick. The warmth of her mouth covers me as her mouth and hand work in tandem. The silky wetness of her tongue working my cock nearly sends me over the edge.

My fingers, with her hair still caught between them, curl into a fist. Reluctantly, I pull her head back, freeing myself from the perfection that is her mouth. But that's not where I want to be right now. This isn't how I want this round to end. She looks up at me, questioning at first, then a flash of self-doubt lights in her eyes.

"You feel so good, babe," I emphasize. "You make me feel like an inexperienced teenage boy again, desperately holding on to his last ounce of restraint in the back seat of the car."

A knowing grin spreads across her face. She remembers that night—the night when we were teenagers and I finally convinced her she'd still be a virgin if we made it to third base. I thought I'd died and gone to heaven when her lips wrapped around my cock for the first time. She was my first...everything, just like I was hers.

"Yeah, I remember that teenage boy and his level of restraint. You didn't warn me what would happen if I didn't stop in time. I still think you did that on purpose."

How could I have been ready to give her up? I'm such a fucking idiot.

"I'll show you what I'm going to do on purpose," I promise and gently push her shoulders back. She slides up the bed, ready and waiting for me.

I bury my face between her legs and waste no time in devouring her. With a swipe of my tongue, I lap up her sweetness. A light graze of my teeth across her clit has her nearly sitting up straight in response. Her nails dig into my scalp, and her fingers pull my hair. When I circle her clit with my tongue and slip my finger inside her wet pussy, her hips lift to meet my attentions, shivers run through her body, and she cries out in pleasure.

This is pure heaven.

Even though I initially resented her insistence over me getting checked out by a doctor, I'm infinitely glad I went through with it right now. That's as far as I'll allow my thoughts of that time to go —it feels like a lifetime ago now, and there's no way in hell I'd go back. Having Grace beneath me, her need for me equaling my need for her, is the only place where I belong. The only place I want to be.

Her greedy mouth claims mine when I settle on top of her. We're skin-to-skin, and I'm taking my time to relish the moments we're reclaiming for ourselves, for our marriage. Her hands slide down my sides, and her fingers grip my ass, giving me a slight tug. I can't help but smile through our kiss—she's not-so-patiently telling me to hurry.

"I can't wait to be inside you," I murmur against her skin as I move my mouth down to her neck. Then to her breast. Her nipple is peaked, a taut bud calling for my attention. My hand cups the underswell of her breast, and my mouth covers her nipple before I draw it fully into my mouth.

"Blake, I need your cock inside me now. Stop depriving me."

Fuck, she still knows exactly how to stoke the fires inside me.

I slip my hand behind her knee and pull her leg up. With our eyes locked, I thrust inside her wet pussy to the hilt. Her fingernails dig into my skin, her neck arches back, and her sexy moan escapes from her lips.

But I completely freeze in place.

I can't move.

Shock has ripped all reasoning from my mind.

She's almost as tight as the first time we made love.

"There hasn't been anyone else for you. Has there?" I already know the answer, but I need to hear the words.

She shakes her head from side to side, but her gaze never strays from mine. The truth is there in the depths of her beautiful emerald green eyes. "No, there hasn't been."

I've never been a crier, but tears sting the back of my eyes when I stare down into hers. Though I betrayed her in the worst fucking way, she never betrayed me. She's remained true this whole time, even knowing what I was doing. Even though she had every right. Even though she knew I planned to ask for a divorce.

"Blake?" she murmurs softly, her eyes questioning me. That burst of insecurity flashes in her gaze again—the doubt I put there.

"I'm just thinking about how I'm the luckiest fucking man alive. Because of you. Whether you're ready to say the words to me again or not, I have to tell you. I love you, Grace. I will tell you every day for the rest of my life. I was lost, but you found me and pulled me back from the edge. You saved me from myself. You're my saving grace."

Tears slide down from the corners of her eyes, across her temples, and disappear into her hairline. She opens her mouth, the words hang on the tip of her tongue, but she stops short of saying them. That's okay, though. I deserve that—and she deserves time. In the meantime, I'll give her every reason to want to say it again. To feel it again.

I release her leg and slide her hands above her head and grind into her. Between the wetness and the softness and the tightness, I use every bit of my focus to keep from ending this way too soon. She becomes my willing rag doll, and I use that to both of our advantages by twisting, turning, bending, moving her into every conceivable position. With every thrust into her sweet pussy, I pour my love and feelings into her. With every grip of my fingers on her hips, I show her how much I love her. With every orgasm that rips through her body, I remind her how much she means to me.

By the time we're both wringing wet with sweat and panting for our next breath, her tears are flowing freely over her cheeks. When we tumble over the edge of ecstasy together, she sobs softly into the crook of my neck. But I know her every sound, her every reaction, her every emotion.

These aren't tears of sorrow.

They're tears of love.

When I finally allow her to leave the bed and my arms, we move to the bathroom together to clean up. The bright light blinds us both for a moment, but when my vision clears, concern fills me and alarm bells ring in my head.

"What the hell happened to your arm, Grace?" Bruises cover the inside of her elbow, all stages of black, purple, green, and yellow.

"It's nothing, Blake. We had some student nurses come through, and I let a couple practice their IV skills on me."

"Did I hurt you just now?"

"No, you didn't hurt me. Well, not my arm anyway. I may have a little trouble walking tomorrow, though."

"I'm sorry, babe, but I don't feel bad about *that* at all."

We laugh together then I sweep her up in my arms to carry her back to bed. Our bed, where I sleep with my arm around her all night, spooning her from behind. Again. Finally.

CHAPTER 12

Grace

*B*lake has slept in my bed...our bed...for the past week, and every night feels better than the last. The way he's held me, made love to me, and whispered how much he loves me when he thinks I'm already asleep has broken down the walls I've tried to keep intact. I can't even lie to myself anymore and say I don't love him. Because I do. So much.

This wasn't part of the plan.

But I can't tell him yet. My heart and mind are still healing— and reeling—from my entire world being turned upside down. I'd already decided to make myself live with him until Kyle was settled into his new routine, but nothing more than that. I'd resigned myself to living in a loveless marriage for the sake of my child. When Kyle left home, it would all be over.

But then the Blake I fell in love with all those years ago had to make a reappearance. In the years we'd grown apart, I'd lost sight of who he really was and what he'd originally wanted out of life. For so long, I didn't realize...*I didn't pay attention*...to what not achieving his dreams did to his self-esteem. The man who tends to my every need, thoroughly satiates my body, and goes out of his way to earn his way back into my heart has accomplished his goal.

But is it too late for me say I love him? Have we missed our chance to be a happy couple? We married young, had Kyle young, and we had looked forward to still being young as empty-nesters. But so much has changed since the dreams of that young couple. So much that can't be changed, regardless of how much we want to do just that.

All these thoughts swirl through my mind when Leigh walks into the room and sits down in front of me with her disapproving look firmly in place. "I bet Blake thinks you're at work today, doesn't he?"

"I am at work today," I reply with a smirk.

"You know what I mean. Don't be a smartass. Grace. *Tell. Him.* Then deal with this like adults. You can't draw this out any longer."

Unfortunately, she's exactly right. That is what has kept me up most nights when he thought I was sound asleep. I don't want to tell him, but I'm out of time to keep it from him any longer.

"He's out of town at a conference until late tonight. He wouldn't even spend one night away from me. He said he's driving home as soon as the meeting is over. I'll tell him tomorrow morning. Scout's honor."

"You were never a scout, so I don't believe that."

"Nurse's honor, then."

"You love him, don't you?" She stares at me incredulously, daring me to even attempt to lie to her.

"I do love him, Leigh. And that makes it even harder to come clean."

"Grace, like it or not, you owe it to him to be honest. Besides that, I'll kick your ass if you don't tell him." She leaves me with her threat, even though we both know she'd be the first person to have my back.

Brent Evers, our hospital's most handsome doctor, takes her seat a few minutes later. He covers my hand with his. "Come by and see me tomorrow when you get a break."

I nod. "Until tomorrow, then."

LEIGH GIVES me the death glare when I step into the unit, but I ignore her and get back to work. By the time our shift is over, I'm so tired I can barely stand up straight. Kyle sent me a text to let me know he and Tracy had a double date with Wes and his girlfriend, so he wouldn't be home until very late. As much as I love my son and love spending time with him, I'm inwardly thankful I'll be home alone for several hours tonight.

I barely remember driving home, but somehow, I make it alive, and I'm now stepping into a hot shower. When I climb into bed, I'm asleep almost as soon as my head hits the pillow. I'm surprised I even feel Blake sliding into bed beside me, but his warmth feels so good against my skin he's impossible to miss.

"Go back to sleep," he whispers. "I'm home, babe."

Before the darkness overtakes me, I hear him whisper into my hair. "I love you, Grace...until the end of time."

The annoyingly loud blaring of the alarm pulls me out my deep sleep. I raise my arm, barely having control over it in my sleep-induced stupor, and slap at the offensive clock. I need the time my snooze button offers this morning. But the ear-piercing blare doesn't stop. Fumbling in the dark, I try pushing different buttons, but nothing works to stop the noise.

Prying my eyelids apart results in something like needles pricking my eyes. I try to blink away the pain and focus on the clock. When I finally wake enough to make out the time on the display, I realize the sound isn't coming from my alarm.

That's the fire alarm.

When I reach over to wake Blake, I realize he's not in the bed with me. What the hell is going on? I throw the covers back and fly out of the bedroom and down the stairs. When I turn the corner to rush into the kitchen, I find Blake at the kitchen table, ignoring the shrieking alarm and choking smoke. The empty griddle is on the stove, the burners are hot, and the cooking oil he used to coat the skillet is smoking, almost at the flash point of a full-fledged fire.

"Blake, what are you doing?" I shriek and run to the stove, grabbing the griddle before the hot oil burns the house down. After I turn the stove off and open the back door to air out the kitchen, I turn back to him. "Blake, what's wrong? Talk to me."

That's when I realize what he's holding in his hands.

The letter I hid under the flour.

Oh. My. God.

Not yet. Not yet. Not yet. I'm not ready to do this. Not now.

His hands shake, and when he looks up at me, I realize he's shaking with rage. His eyes are narrowed into barely there slits. His handsome face is contorted in anger. But I know the calm timbre of his voice is a façade, shrouding the volcano simmering just beneath the surface.

"It was really late when I got home last night. I drove for hours to get back home to you, to hold you for as long as I could. You were knocked out when I got here, so I tried not to wake you when I slid into the bed with you. How stupid am I, Grace? The last week I've spent back in our bed after nearly a year of being out of it gave me a kind of hope I haven't had in years. Hope that, finally, we would be a real *couple*—sharing everything, growing closer, getting better with age. I lay awake for hours after I got home, thinking about how much I love you. How much my heart has swelled with love for you over the past several weeks. How we seemed to have found our stride and, Grace, I've been ready to hit the ground running with that.

"So, I got up before your alarm went off to make you pancakes for breakfast. I wanted to do something nice for you before you leave for work today. I wanted to surprise you."

He stands, the letter still gripped in his fist, and the volcano erupts. The calm veneer cracks, and he begins to shout. "But I'm the one who was in for the surprise, wasn't I? All this time, I've done everything in my power to win back your love. I've played the whipped dog. I've been the loving husband. I've been the dominant lover. I've tried to satisfy you in every way I know possible. But this whole time, you've been keeping this in your back pocket, haven't you?

"Let me guess, Grace. Your plan was to make me fall in love with you again. Completely and totally head over heels in fucking love with you, to the point I can't fucking breathe without you. Then you use this as your ultimate 'Fuck you, Blake.' Is this your way to pay me back for Tammy? Because this is really fucking cruel, Grace. Here I thought you were beginning to love me again. I never imagined you were capable of going to such lengths to destroy me."

He turns his back to me, but I can still tell he's raking his hand across his face. His hand stops, covering his mouth. He leans against the back doorframe, staring outside into the darkness of the way too early morning. Silent. Hurt.

But he's as far off the mark as east is from west when it comes to judging my intentions. He's not thinking rationally—he's reacting out of pain and fear, much the same way I reacted when I first found out about him and Tammy. Now that I've waited and he found out this way instead of from me directly, I'll have a harder time convincing him otherwise.

But I have to try.

"Blake," I say calmly. Yelling back at him right now will only escalate this further into a huge fight that I don't have the energy for this morning. "Listen to me, and listen closely. You're wrong about everything—about me, about why I haven't told you about this, about me using it to hurt you. If you'll just think about what I've done so far, you'll understand."

He turns and fixes me with a cold, expressionless stare. The warmth and love he gave me just yesterday are nowhere to be found now. Painful jabs stab my heart, and tears sting my eyes. "By all means, do explain. I'm all ears."

"When I first confirmed you were cheating on me with Tammy, I went to the doctor. Even though you hadn't touched me in months, I insisted he test me for STDs because I wasn't one hundred percent sure how long you'd been seeing her. While I was there, I had my full yearly checkup to get it out of the way.

"He felt a lump in my breast during my examination."

Blake's face softens a little, barely enough for anyone else to see, but I do.

"Of course, he told me not to worry, a lot of medical processes can cause lumps. Still, he didn't want to wait to check it out. So I had a mammogram. Then an ultrasound. Then a biopsy. With each test, I knew what the diagnosis would be before the results were ever given to me. What I didn't know, and couldn't have guessed, was that the pathology report would say it's triple-negative breast cancer, though.

"Because it's an aggressive form of breast cancer, and the treatment is also aggressive, I had to reprioritize everything in my life. I took a long, hard look in the mirror and realized there were things I had to change. The main thing was your relationship with Kyle."

"I don't understand." Anger is now replaced by confusion. And a hint of fear.

"The day that letter arrived, confirming the type of cancer beyond a shadow of a doubt, was the day you were going to ask me for a divorce. My private investigator had already overheard your conversations with Tammy about it. If I had agreed to the divorce and just let you go, Kyle never would've forgiven you,

Blake. When I'm gone, you'll be all he has, and he'll need you to be there for him.

"The only way I could convince you to stay at that point was for Kyle, because I knew you still loved him no matter what had happened between us. I knew you'd want what's best for him. The nine months was for you and Kyle to reconnect not only as father and son, but as friends. I did that so he wouldn't hate you for leaving me when I was dying of cancer, Blake. None of this was to hurt you—I've been trying to help you."

"Nine months? Is that your prognosis? Is that all the time we have left with you?" The pain in his eyes is killing me inside. I wish I could take it away. I wish I could tell him I have years and years left to live. But the truth is...

"I don't know how much time I have left, Blake. I've been seeing an oncologist. We're trying to shrink the tumor enough to remove it surgically without removing my entire breast. We may not be successful with that, though, but I've had two chemo-therapy treatments so far. My first one was when you came home from the snowboarding trip early. The medications knocked me on my ass—I had zero energy left to do anything. The second round was just yesterday."

Blake sits down at the table. His gaze never leaves mine, but I can tell he's having a hard time processing all the information I'm throwing at him. I've lived it for the past three or four months, and it's still hard for me to process.

"Why were you so tired and losing weight before your first treatment?"

"Mainly stress. Waiting for the results of the tests and the biopsy had me on pins and needles. Worrying about the future and how I was going to handle everything really took a toll on me."

"But I knew nothing about any of it." His tone is rueful as he rakes his hands over his face.

"I swear, I was going to tell you everything today, Blake. When

I first asked for the time and the promises, I had no idea our relationship would take such a turn. My only thought was of you and Kyle. That was also why I agreed to have Christmas with my parents—to put our disagreements behind us and make sure you and Kyle are set for the future."

"I don't understand."

"The three envelopes I brought home Christmas night? They're the legal documents for trust funds they set up for you, Kyle, and me. I took them to a financial advisor and invested the money so you two won't ever have to worry about making ends meet again. Everything is taken care of, Blake. I don't know why you'd think I'd use this to hurt you. I'm trying to help you by thinking of your future."

His eyes drop to the letter he still holds in his hand. The letter confirming my biopsy results. The letter that effectively sealed our fate when the pathologist sealed the envelope with the findings inside.

Stage IIB triple negative breast cancer with axillary lymph node involvement.

"You're thinking of and planning for *my* future," he says quietly, "when you don't even know if you'll be in it."

He folds his arms on the table in front of him then leans over, burying his face in the bend of his elbow. When his shoulders begin to shake, my heart shatters inside my chest like fine crystal dropped on a marble countertop. I rush to his side and wrap my arms around him. I know the hopelessness and helplessness he feels right now all too well. Time can't help us to accept it either. Time is a luxury we may not have much of at this stage of the game.

But I give him several minutes to absorb what I've shared, what he's read, and what it all means to our little family. For this small amount of time, I just hold him close to me and let him feel

115

my touch. Rubbing my hand across his back. Running my fingers through his hair. Placing kisses on the side of his head. Letting him feel my love while he comes to terms with his grief.

Then he quickly turns, wraps his arms around my waist and squeezes me. He drops to his knees on the floor, still holding on to me. When he looks up at me, his eyes are bloodshot from his tears, but his love for me shines brightly again. "I should've been there when you had the first inkling something was wrong. I should've been with you through every test and procedure. You never should've had to go through this alone. I'm so sorry, Grace. Please forgive me. Swear to me you're doing everything you can to fight this. Promise me you'll never give up fighting to beat it, Grace. I can't face the future without you. I don't even want to try."

"I've already forgiven you, Blake. I wouldn't be sleeping with you every night if I hadn't. I promise you, I'll never stop trying or give up fighting this. But you have to accept there's a possibility you will have to go on without me. You'll have to be strong for Kyle. We'll tell him together—and soon. The chemotherapy cocktail I'm on has basically a one hundred percent guarantee I'll lose all my hair in the next couple of days since I just finished my second treatment. It's not like I'll be able to hide the side effects of the treatments any longer. I'd rather you both be prepared for the worst and hope for the best, and act normal until we know something for sure...one way or another."

He nods solemnly. "I'll be here for you every step of the way. There's nothing I won't do for you, babe. You'll never have to endure a moment of this journey alone again."

CHAPTER 13

Blake

While Grace showers, I air out the kitchen and replay the entire morning in my mind. Knowing she had to leave for work early this morning, I slipped out of bed before her to make our breakfast so we'd at least have a few minutes together. With the pan and the oil heating up, I grabbed the ingredients to whip up pancakes. When I pulled the bag of flour out of the airtight container, I saw something fall out of the corner of my eye, but I didn't pay much attention to it at first.

But once I picked it up, the letter had my full attention.

The doctor's name in the return address wasn't familiar to me.

It was addressed to Grace.

She'd hidden it in the flour canister.

My first thought was admittedly that she'd been cheating on me, after all. So I snatched the letter from the envelope, ready to tear into a doctor for trying to take my wife from me.

Then I read the pathology report. Then I read it again. And again. Over and over until the words finally started to sink in and make sense to my muddled brain.

A doctor isn't taking my wife away from me.

Cancer is.

I don't know how long I stared at the diagnosis while all the thoughts ran through my mind at Mach speed. Reading it didn't answer any of my questions—the most prevalent one being why Grace hid this from me for so long. We've been working on our relationship and our marriage for weeks and weeks now.

Haven't we?

It started out as an agreement, but a little time together proved to be exactly what we needed to reconnect as a couple.

Didn't it?

The only logical answer I could come up with to answer both questions was one simple word.

No.

No, we hadn't been working on our relationship. I had been—but she'd been pretending.

No, we hadn't reconnected as a couple. I had reconnected with her—but she hadn't with me.

It was why she still hadn't told me she loved me even though I've said it to her a hundred times now.

I foolishly thought she'd kept it from me because I'd betrayed her and she wanted to retaliate. What better way to get the last word than to make me fall head over heels in love with her again, only to make me look and feel like a fool in the end? I'd ended my relationship with Tammy. My job had been on the line. My whole world had turned, and Grace had become my primary focus.

The pain from just the thought of her betrayal crushed the life out of me. Pains shot through my chest. Tears stung my eyes. I wanted to yell for her, to demand the answers I didn't want to hear, but I couldn't speak. My whole world was crashing and burning all around me, and there wasn't a fucking thing I could do to stop it.

Then she was there in the kitchen with me, and every insane thought in my mind suddenly tumbled out of my mouth. I don't even know if everything I said was in full, coherent sentences. Through the accusations I hurled at her, and after the way I shut down in a poor attempt to protect my heart from more damage, my Grace still put me first. Though I was a complete ass, she patiently explained what had happened.

Never again, I vowed right then and there. Never again will I think of myself before I think of my wife.

Everything she'd done was for Kyle and me. She put us first when the concentration should've been on her. All the concerted efforts should've been to heal her. That shouldn't have surprised me, in retrospect. That's who she's always been, from the time we started dating as teenagers until now.

After thirty-eight years, I should be wiser than I am. I thought I'd have life figured out by now. This news explains why I've seen tears in her eyes from time to time, though she tried to hide it. This whole time, I thought her tears were only because of my infidelity. Now I know she carried so much more weight on her shoulders than I realized.

My attention turns to her as she comes back down the stairs. Her sniffles are muffled, but I hear them just the same. She lowers her head and wipes away a tear, trying to hide her concerns from me again. But I can't take my eyes off of her now. The irrational fear that this moment is the last I'll have with her has overpowered my rational mind. Logic has been replaced by absurdity. The truth is I don't care how ludicrous I appear to anyone else—I know I can't live without her. I'm just a dark shell of a man without her love and light in my life.

Saving Grace is my only hope.

"No more hiding from me, Grace. Talk to me, babe. Why are you crying? What are you feeling, thinking, worrying about? Let me help carry the burden."

When she looks up at me, the dam breaks, and streams of tears cover her cheeks. "It's already started."

"What's already started?" I open my arms, and she flies into them, wrapping her arms around my waist. With my mouth close to her ear, I rub her back with one hand while holding her close with the other. "Talk to me, my love. Tell me what's going on."

"In the shower," she sobs. "My hair started falling out in clumps. God, Blake, it's already starting, and I'm not ready for this."

"I know, babe. But believe me when I say it'll be okay. I can't even imagine what a hard adjustment this is for you, but it won't change how much I love you."

"What about..." She stops for a second to collect her courage and swallow her weeping. "What if they have to remove my breast? I won't look the same at all. My hair, my body, nothing."

"Hey, listen to me for a minute." She nods her head but doesn't raise her face to look at me. "I'm sorry this is happening to you, and I'm sorry you have more to face in the near future. But I want you to remember something when you're sad or worried about the coming changes."

"What?" she asks with a watery voice.

"Your hair is beautiful, but I don't love it. I didn't marry you for your body. Our vows didn't include anything about your appearance. If your hair never grows back, I won't care one bit about it. If it grows back completely gray, I still won't care. If it's long, short, blond, red, brown, black, or pink, I don't care.

"I'm in love with *you*. Not your hair, not your body. I love everything about you, but any changes you go through won't change my love for *you*. If the doctor says you need a mastectomy, I'll ask him about a double mastectomy so we'll never have to face this again. After the surgery, I'll tell you every day how beautiful you are to me, because it's not about how you look on the outside. It's about who you are inside—and you're the most beautiful woman ever to walk on Earth. I'm sorry I ever made you doubt it."

She cries into my chest, and all I can do is hold her until she finishes. I can repeat myself until I'm blue in the face, but actions speak louder than words, and she needs rock-solid proof. I'm ready to be whatever she needs me to be. For however long she'll have me.

When she finally looks up at me, her eyes are red and puffy from crying, but she's still gorgeous. "I'd better get going, or I'll be late for work. Dr. Evers, my oncologist, asked me to come by his office today on my break. I'm afraid he has more bad news for me."

"What time? I'll be there with you."

"I can go during lunch if you want to meet me."

"Lunch it is. I'll bring you something to eat because I know you won't take the time to grab anything." She smiles sheepishly at me but doesn't disagree. "Come on, I'll take you to work and get you breakfast at the drive-thru since I made you miss pancakes this morning."

We hold hands the entire ride to the hospital, both of us searching for the strength to make it through the day. At least we're reaching for each other through this crisis. Before she gets out, I lean across the console and pull her to me. Our lips lock in a demanding kiss, then I feel her tongue sweep across my bottom lip. Without hesitation, I wrap my tongue around hers and suck it into my mouth. My fingers curl around her neck and dig in, while being mindful not to tug on her hair.

"I'll see you in a few hours," I say when we break for air. "I love you, Grace. Until the end of time."

She kisses me softly and says she'll text me her lunch time when she checks the break schedule in the unit. Then she slides out of the car, and I watch her walk across the courtyard to the front door of the hospital.

When I get home, I find Kyle in the kitchen flipping the pancakes I never got around to making. "You'd sleep through an earthquake, wouldn't you?"

"Maybe. But not through the fire alarm that was going off way before dawn this morning. I thought I'd find burned food everywhere, but it doesn't seem the food ever made it to the stove." Kyle arches one eyebrow when he turns his gaze to me.

"No, I never poured the first pancake. Have a seat, son. We need to talk."

He stops what he's doing and looks me dead in the eye. "How bad is Mom's cancer?"

I'm so shocked, all I can do is stare at him with my mouth gaping open for several seconds. "You already knew?"

What the fuck? Am I the only one who didn't know?

"Yeah, I heard her on the phone when she got the ultrasound results. When they did the biopsy, I made sure I was here more to help her around the house while she was healing. She didn't tell me, so I didn't ask. I figured she'd tell me when she was ready or knew more about it." He takes the seat across from me and puts the plate of pancakes between us.

"It's serious, Kyle. She's on chemotherapy now to try to reduce the size of the tumor before having surgery. She's already losing her hair, and she said it'll all be gone within a couple of days. I'll be straight with you, son. She's not taking that part too well."

"This is why we went to see her parents for Christmas?"

"Yes, it is." I nod and look down, not wanting to speak the rest of my thoughts.

"She's making her end-of-life arrangements, isn't she?"

"What? What did you say?" I can't breathe.

"I read about it after I overheard her conversation—I think she was talking to Leigh. Mom said she wouldn't put the pressure on us to make her final healthcare decisions, that we'd have enough on us without having to understand all the medical lingo. I think she's making a living will or whatever it's called to spell out her final wishes."

We sit in painful silence for a couple of minutes. Neither of us moving. Neither reaching for the stack of pancakes.

"Dad, is Mom going to die?"

I shake my head, but I can't say the word. Because I don't

know. I'm not sure I know everything yet. I'm not sure if Grace even knows everything yet. I have so many questions for the doctor today, I don't even know what to ask. My only clear thought is to beg him to save my wife.

Don't take her away from me now. Please, God.

"Are you not telling me something?" Kyle demands.

"You know everything I know, son. We're still just reeling from the news. I'm going to the doctor with her in a few hours. Hopefully I'll find out more then."

"How am I supposed to go to school with all this on my mind?"

"You know your mom hasn't told you about this just for that very reason. She wants your mind on your grades and where you're going to college. She wants you to focus on your life and your goals."

"I don't give a shit if this makes me sound like a mama's boy. There's no way I'm leaving my mom and going far away for college when she has cancer. I will stay right here and go to a local college until she gets the all clear. I'll take a year off, find a part-time job, and help around here. Whatever it takes. But if she's fighting for her life, I won't miss out on spending that time with her."

"That doesn't make you sound like a mama's boy at all. And, so what if it did? You love her, as you should. She'll probably still try to argue with you, though."

"She won't win that fight." He stabs a pancake with his fork and covers it with syrup. "But I'm not going to school today. I won't be able to focus on anything but what the doctor has to say. You'll tell me, right?"

"I will tell you. And I'll talk to your mother about keeping you informed, too. No more secrets in this house."

Kyle looks at me as if he wants to say something more, but he nods his head and begins eating instead. The kid is more observant than I gave him credit for, so my gut says he wanted to ask me about Tammy and the secrets I've kept. But shame and regret keep me from confessing my sins. The fear of losing my son and my wife is far too real.

The morning drags by despite the numerous phone calls I've made and browser tabs I have open, researching every possible scenario. There's a reason all my doctors are adamant that their patients refrain from using the internet to self-diagnose. I'm almost convinced *I'm* dying of a rare disease only contracted in the remote areas of Africa, where I've never been, just from reading the various symptoms listed.

Grace sent me a quick text with the time to meet her at Dr. Evers's office, so I leave early and pick up her lunch on the way. I don't know how I expect her to eat when my stomach is rolling like huge waves in a hurricane. The unknown is driving me crazy. With a clearer picture of what we're facing, I think Grace and I can find a way to beat this. Together.

Grace is already in the waiting room when I step into the doctor's office. I rush to her side and offer the bag with her lunch. She stares at it for a moment as if it's an insect she doesn't want to touch, but she eventually takes it from me and places it in the empty chair beside her.

"Not hungry?" I ask, even though I know the answer.

"I couldn't eat now if my life depended on it." She chuckles lightly for a second, then suddenly stops when the weight of her words hits us each squarely in the chest. "Bad choice of words, I guess."

"Grace, do you know something I don't?"

"No, I don't know anything for certain. I just have a bad feeling all the side effects from the chemo I've had aren't actually side effects from chemo."

"Grace Hardy?" The nurse calls from the open doorway before I can press her for more information.

The nurse takes Grace's vitals and records her weight, and the full reality of her drastic weight loss over the past couple of months hits me. It wasn't only because of me, but now I wish that wasn't the case. My feet are rooted to the floor when the nurse starts to lead Grace to the doctor's office, not an examination room. My heart is racing, my legs are jumping, and my hands are shaking.

This isn't happening.

CHAPTER 14

Grace

When Brent told me to come see him today, I thought it was for a standard checkup after starting this round of chemotherapy. When his nurse escorts me to his office instead of a patient room, I can't help but think more bad news awaits me. As if I haven't had enough. As if I'm not already devastated just thinking about missing Kyle's college graduation.

Somehow, I make my feet move and absently follow the nurse, until I realize Blake isn't beside me. When I turn to look for him, I know he senses it too. His face is pale white, almost ghostly. His lips are parted, and he's breathing rapidly—too rapidly. He's about to hyperventilate. Unfortunately, I know exactly how he feels. That's how I felt after the initial confirmation the tumor was malignant. Then again when the axillary lymph node involvement was confirmed. I am grateful it wasn't a distant lymph node, though. No metastasis to distant organs is a good sign.

After I turn and walk back to him, I take his hand in mine and squeeze it until he looks down at me. He's still so handsome—age has only made him more attractive. With my thoughts focused on him, I calm my speeding heart and slow my breathing, projecting peace and composure for his sake.

"Blake, take slow, deep breaths before you pass out on me," I say quietly. "I don't know if I can do this alone. Right now, I really need you by my side."

The cloudy confusion in his eyes clears, and he sees me standing in front of him at last. He nods, and though his chin quivers, he puts on a brave face. "Until the end of time."

We stroll together down the hall on what feels like the longest walk of my life. The door that seems so far away, yet not far enough, because I still have to walk through it and face what's waiting for me in there. The unknown, unseen monster hiding in the dark, waiting to devour me and all my dreams in one fatal swoop.

Maybe Blake had the right idea. Passing out right about now is way too appealing.

We take our seats in front of the big oak desk and wait for the doctor to join us. The folders sitting on top of his desk tempt me almost past my capacity for rational thought. If mine is in that stack, all the answers I need are just *right there*. The only reason I'm not rifling through them right now is because it's ethically wrong, and illegal, for me to see another patient's chart. Oh, and because the door to the office is standing wide open, so I'd get caught red-handed anyway.

"What side effects?" Blake asks, pulling me from my plan to close the door and help myself.

"What?" My brows draw down, completing my confused expression.

"You said you thought your side effects were something else. What are your symptoms?"

I don't want to tell him. Not because I'm hiding them, but because I don't want to give those nagging thoughts a platform. But I vowed to face this disease head on, and this is just one part of it. "I've had some chest pains and a cough. But that could be from a compromised immune system."

"It could," he agrees solemnly. Without conviction. Without moving his eyes from mine. Without hiding the emotions swirling in his thoughts.

"Sorry to keep you both waiting," Brent says as he rushes in from behind us and closes the door. He takes a seat behind his desk and unlocks the filing cabinet drawer to retrieve my file. Of course it wouldn't be lying out in the open, and I would've been caught trying to find it.

With my file open on his desk, he studies the results a little too long for it to be good news. I close my eyes and squeeze Blake's hand. He squeezes back, sharing my fear and sharing his strength.

"Just tell me, Brent. I know you're trying to find a way to say it."

"Spoken like a true ICU nurse, Grace." He smiles, but it's a sad smile. "Your dry cough during treatment concerned me, so I asked a colleague to pull your scan from last week for another look and to send me the results as soon as possible. I'm sorry to tell you, Grace, but we're no longer looking for a cure. Your breast cancer has metastasized to your right lung. As you know, once breast cancer moves to a distant organ, that changes everything. We're no longer treating BC. We have to focus on mBC and what that means for your treatment long term."

Our grips tighten simultaneously. Blake's provides the anchor that keeps me tethered to my body. Otherwise, I'd float away in what already feels like an out-of-body experience. Is this a dream, or is this real? I can't feel anything, yet I feel everything.

"How long do I have before it's past the point of no return, Brent?" That's my voice, but I have no idea how I asked the question when my brain clearly isn't operating.

He looks uncomfortable. When an oncologist looks uncomfortable, it's impossible to have a positive outlook.

"You know I can't tell you that, Grace. We'll continue your

course of chemotherapy for this regimen then determine surgical options for removal of the tumor from your breast after this round is finished. We have to see how the tumor responds to these drugs. There are several nodules in your lung that the chemotherapy will treat and hopefully stabilize. After you've healed from the surgery, you'll need radiation, and we'll decide our course for the next round of chemotherapy."

"I need to clarify something. You said BC and mBC. What does that mean?" Blake asks.

"I'm sorry—occupational hazard of treating nurses. mBC is metastatic breast cancer, and BC is breast cancer."

"So the positive axillary lymph node isn't considered metastatic?"

"No, not the axillary lymph nodes. That's still considered the breast area and is actually quite frequent. If it showed up in a lymph node in her groin, for example, that would be metastatic. In this case, the cancer has already spread to her lung, changing her original diagnosis of breast cancer to metastatic breast cancer, or mBC for short. You may also hear it called de novo metastatic breast cancer. That just means it had already metastasized when she was diagnosed."

The occupational hazard of being a nurse under treatment is I know far too well how to read what *is* said...and what *isn't* said.

When I glance over at Blake, I can tell he wants to ask more questions. The vague "wait and see" approach doesn't mesh well with his need to fix everything *right now*. But he can't do anything about this situation.

No cure exists for this advanced disease. There are only treatments that will hopefully prevent the tumors from growing or spreading more. Had we caught it sooner, my odds would've been much better.

He doesn't yet realize he can't save me.

He can't cure me.

He can't make the cancer go away.

The only guarantee in this entire ambiguous scenario is this monster will one day kill me.

My triple-negative diagnosis renders targeted therapy outside of clinical trials useless.

How do I tell my husband and my son that I'm going to die?

"We can get a second opinion, Grace. They missed this in the first scan—it could've been misread this time," Blake insists.

I shake my head. "I don't need a second opinion, Blake. I know they're right. The chest pains, the dry cough. It makes sense."

"Grace, taking some time off work now isn't a bad idea. I've just dumped a lot on your shoulders. You could do without the stress of working in ICU for a few days." Brent has good intentions, but his suggestion feels a lot like he's telling me to get my affairs in order as soon as possible.

"Maybe you're right."

"I can call down to Human Resources and tell them I'm taking you out of work right now. They can get someone from the ER to cover the rest of your shift," Brent offers.

"Grace, take him up on this. I think we both need some time to absorb everything we just heard," Blake requests. "Kyle knows about your breast cancer. He overheard you talking to Leigh. He needs to know about this too. Our family needs this time, babe."

"Okay, yes. Whatever you think." I need to let go of the reins and allow Blake to take control. I'm only hanging on to my stability by a thread as it is, and there's nothing I can do to stop that strand from unraveling.

Brent picks up the phone on his desk and calls HR himself, without delegating the task to his staff to handle. Blake and I stare at each other wordlessly as Brent stresses the importance of approving my immediate leave. When he hangs up, I've been approved for leave through my next treatment, a month away. He says he'll have them extend it if I need additional time.

Blake and I thank Brent for his help and leave the office, both of us steeped in a heavy fog. After I grab my purse from the nurses' station and promise to call Leigh later, Blake and I leave together. I can't voice the words at the moment, but I'm so glad he drove me to work and was here with me when I received this terrible news. He doesn't have to say or do anything to console me —just having him by my side makes all the difference.

Blake doesn't release my hand until we arrive at home and he's forced to let go so I can get out of the car. Once we're inside, I make it as far as the kitchen before he grabs me, turns me to face him, then buries me in his embrace. My cheek is flat against his chest, my arms are around his waist, and I feel safe and protected in his arms. We stand like this for several minutes, not moving, not talking, just feeling—exuding our own unspoken fears and uncertainties while trying to soothe the other's. The usual yin and yang, give and take, and push and pull any couple experiences... multiplied by a thousand.

Though we're reluctant to, we finally release each other so we can face what lies ahead. I step to the sliding glass door, watching the snow fall, and rest my forehead against the cool glass. The fire pit in the backyard has been cleared of all the recent snow, and a sharp pang hits my chest. But the pain isn't from the cancer, it's from a broken heart. The pavers and fire pit were a gift for Blake, something I knew he'd wanted for a long time, but there was more behind my decision.

"You can call me crazy if you want, but I can feel your feelings, Grace. It's like they're shooting out of you and straight into me. Talk to me. Tell me what you're thinking. Don't hold it all in and carry this alone anymore."

I can't face him when I say this. I'm just not ready yet. "Okay, but you won't like it."

"I can take it."

"I was just thinking about when I had the fire pit installed for your Christmas present. That was the primary reason I did it. But I had another reason too."

"And what was that reason?"

"Triple negative breast cancer has a higher recurrence rate than the other types, over time. I thought the patio would be a good selling feature for the house if the cancer returned later, but you'd be able to enjoy it until then. I just never considered this turn of events. I thought I had more time."

"Mom? What's going on?" The confusion and concern in Kyle's voice rip my heart to shreds.

I don't want to have this conversation.

But it can't wait any longer.

Time is an unknown commodity I can't take for granted anymore.

I turn to face them, no longer hiding my emotions. "You two have a seat. We need to have a family meeting."

My nerves are completely shot, and I anxiously run my hands up my face and through my hair. My fingers come out with clusters of my hair wrapped around them. While shaking uncontrollably, I walk to the garbage can and watch the tufts of hair slip through my fingers. When I turn toward Blake and Kyle, I find their eyes are still transfixed on the garbage can, though the lid is closed.

"We'll all have to get used to seeing that over the next few days," I say as I sit. "Kyle, your dad told me you know some of what's going on. But I'm afraid I have more bad news to share with you. A few months ago, I found out that I have breast cancer. Alone, that diagnosis was bad enough, but manageable through a course of chemotherapy and probably several weeks of radiation therapy. But, it turns out I was originally misdiagnosed.

"The cancer isn't only in my breast, it's also in my lung. Since it has already spread, my condition is more advanced than we first thought. There's something you both have to understand about this change in diagnosis, and I can't sugarcoat it because we all have to face the terrible truth about it. There's more to it than just extending my chemotherapy and making it go away. There is no cure for metastatic breast cancer."

Kyle stares blankly at me for several heartbeats. I know how he feels. Absorbing this is harder than I ever imagined. For a seventeen-year-old to understand the implications is asking a lot.

"There's no cure? What does that mean, Grace?"

When my tears spill over onto my cheeks, Blake leans back in his chair and releases a haggard gasp.

"It means, at some point, this cancer will kill me."

"How long are we talking, Mom?" Kyle's question is asked on a whisper, as if he's afraid to speak the words aloud.

"Some women live two to three years with it. Some women have lived more than five years with it. Others have lived anywhere from ten to twenty years. There are so many variables with metastasis, it's impossible to even guess right now."

The silence around the table is deafening. They don't know what to say, and I can appreciate that. Platitudes are not what any of us needs right now. This subject is depressing. The outlook is grim. And my ability to maintain my composure is waning.

"Guys, I know this is a lot to take in. Frankly, I need some time to try to process what all of it means myself. I'm going upstairs to be alone for a while."

"You promised you wouldn't give up," Blake reminds me.

"I'm not giving up. I'm just...regrouping. When I come back down, we're all going to go about our day as usual."

Kyle stands and wraps his arms around me.

My big, strong boy is crying like a baby.

Dear God, please help me be strong. For my son's sake, don't let me fall apart in front of him.

"Hey," I say softly. "I'm not giving up, so you're not giving up. No matter what happens, everything will be okay, baby."

He squeezes me tighter and nods his head. Before he releases me, he kisses me on the cheek. I know he's saying he loves me through his gesture because speaking the words would release the fears he's trying to hold at bay. I return the notion with a kiss on his cheek then walk upstairs to have my breakdown in private.

CHAPTER 15

Blake

*T*here's no cure.

That's why she asked Dr. Evers how long she has before she's past the point of no return. The point where the treatment no longer works and the only recourse is to keep her comfortable until the end.

"Kyle." I wait for him to look up at me. "There's something I need to do for your mom. I need your help."

"Anything."

"Wait here. I'll be right back."

When I come back into the kitchen, Kyle inspects the items I'm carrying, and instant understanding crosses his face. "In that case, I need your help with the same thing."

I nod, so proud of the young man we've raised, and hand him the clippers. After I'm seated, I drape the towel around my shoulders. "Take it all off, please."

With the clippers plugged in, he flips the switch and goes to work shaving my head. Grace faced all the pointing fingers, judging eyes, and hateful sneers alone when she was pregnant in high school—as much from her own parents as the other kids in school. She won't face the stares and questioning looks of her baldness alone. As long as she doesn't have hair, neither will I.

When he finishes shaving me, we switch places, and I grab a fresh towel for him. "Are you sure you want to do this too?"

"I'm positive. And I dare anyone to say a word about it."

After we clean up the hair from the floor, we move to the guest bathroom to finish what we've started. Standing in front of the dual sink vanity, we lather our heads with shaving cream and remove the remaining stubble. Clean-shaven and wiped dry, we admire each other for a moment before Kyle hugs me.

It's been so long since my son hugged me.

Too long.

"This is the worst I've ever felt. But we're a family, and we stick together."

"Absolutely, son. Until the end of time."

Kyle and I retreat to the den and mindlessly watch TV. At first, he asked a few more questions about Grace's condition, but he's been quiet since then. We've alternated crying while respecting the other's privacy. We're both going through our private hell, but neither of us feels much like talking about it more than we already have.

I don't know about him, but I have no idea what's happened in the movie we've been watching for the past two hours. All I can think about is what Grace is doing up there alone. Even though the wait has been almost too much to bear, I've given her privacy and time to think about herself. My insecurities keep playing tricks on my mind.

I've tried to put myself in her shoes. How would I react if I received a death sentence? Would I want time alone, or would I want to lean on her and listen as she tells me everything will be all right?

Then I realize I'm being selfish because I want her with me. Every second of every day, I want her by my side. Is that too much to ask? Yes, it is, because she asked me to give her the time alone.

As much as I want to walk beside her every step of the way, there will be one step I can't take with her. She'll face it alone, regardless of how badly I don't want it to happen. And that's the step she's trying to come to terms with now.

Another hour passes before I hear her footsteps on the stairs. She keeps a slow pace, the weight of the world still weighing her down.

"Okay, so is there anything you two want to go do?" she asks as she walks toward the den, forcing a smile in her voice.

Then she steps into the room, and her bottom jaw drops to her chest. Her hands fly to her face to cover her mouth, and tears spring to her eyes. Her gaze darts between Kyle and me, taking in our bald heads. Our gesture of love for her.

"Oh my God. What have you two done?" she asks with a watery voice.

"We're with you, Grace. Until the end of time." I stand and meet her halfway across the room. She rushes into my arms and partly cries, partly laughs. Kyle joins us, wrapping one arm around my shoulders and one around hers.

"I guess one of you should shave my head now. I'd rather get it over with all at once than to find another cluster of hair on my pillow."

"I'll give you the buzz cut. Dad can shave the stubble off. We'll be triplets, then."

"Let's do it now. I'm ready."

She surprises me when she doesn't shed one tear over the long locks of brown hair that fall to the floor. With each pass of the clippers, I'm there to sweep them up and whisk them away. She doesn't need the visual reminder of seeing the pile of hair beneath her. In the bathroom, I sit her on a stool and cover her head in shaving cream. After every swipe of the blade, I kiss her, reminding her that my love endures regardless of the circumstance.

After I clean her completely bald head with a warm washcloth, she stands and faces me. She tries to hide her uncertainty when she looks up at me, but that quickly disappears when I smile lovingly before giving her a passionate kiss.

"Time for our selfie," Kyle calls from the door and waves his phone.

We gather together, and Kyle snaps our picture—three bald heads with three thankful smiles.

"Did you have any great revelations in our bedroom?"

"I did. Let's go back into the den, and I'll fill you both in."

Kyle and I take our seats while Grace paces back and forth in front of us.

"I've seen my share of death and tragedy in the ICU. I've had my heart broken for patients and their families. The one question that I've heard the most over the years is why him or why her, and I've never had a suitable answer to give them. But today when I asked why me, I realized the answer to my own question.

"Why *not* me? I can't wish this on someone else. I can't wish it away. I'm no better than any of the other women who have endured and suffered through this. So, even though I hate it, and I would cure it if I could, I've decided to look at this as a gift. Because it has made me realize and appreciate things I've just taken for granted."

"Like what? What could possibly make you think this is a gift?" I'm shocked and can't hide my reaction. This isn't a gift—it's a fucking curse. It's robbing me of the love of my life. I'm not sure if she's serious or if she has snapped. If I'm honest, I'd have to say it's an even split.

"Like time, for example. I've always taken an abundance of time for granted. There's always tomorrow. One day. Someday. Next year. Sometime. We've always said we'd go on a tour of Italy, before Venice is completely underwater, but we never went.

We've put off going ice skating on the pond just down the road because we have a long winter and can go anytime. Doing what we want to do hasn't been a priority.

"Now, *time* is a priority because it's limited. If there's something we want to do, we should find a way to do it—as soon as possible. If not now, then when? I started making a list of things I want to do while I'm still able to enjoy them."

"Mom...you're already making a bucket list?" Kyle sounds crushed, and I don't blame him. I'm having a hard time with this myself.

"I'm not calling it that. I hit the big-ticket items first—the ones most everyone would list. Skydiving, for the thrill of cheating death and laughing in its face. A cruise around the world to see all the sites I've never been able to see before. Things like that. Then I read my list, and at first, I thought some of them were just silly, and I asked myself why I even listed them. I started to cross them off, but then I stopped and asked a different question.

"Why not? Big or little, silly or meaningful, all of these things make up our lives and who we are. They're all equally important. Building memories with each other is what's most important. So, I'm calling it my 'why not' list instead of a bucket list."

"Can we see this list?" I'm really curious what else she has listed.

"Yes, you can. But first, I want you both to make your own 'why not' list. What do you want to do but haven't made time for it? And I don't want you to list things you think I want to do. This is for both of you, too. We'll make memories together, doing things we each want to do, and having fun while we can."

"I don't like when you say 'while we can,' Mom. It makes me think you're dying tomorrow."

"We don't know how much time any of us has left, Kyle. A car wreck could kill me before the cancer does. But knowing this is inside me has made me so much more aware of that fact. So I don't want to waste one more second waiting to do anything I really want to do. Or anything you or your daddy want to do. If there's anything on my list either of you doesn't want to do, that's okay, too. I can do it by myself and tell you all about it later."

"Nope, I'm going with you. No matter what you want to do, I want to do it too. I'll be with you every step of the way." Every memory she wants to create, I want to be part of it. I'll need those memories one day.

She walks over to me and sits in my lap. Having her close feels so good—I could hold her like this for the rest of my life and be content. She leans in, her hands on my face, and presses her lips against mine. "I'm glad you said that, because I want you with me in everything I do. And I want to be with you in whatever you want to do."

"What's the first item on your list for tonight? We'll make it happen, babe."

"It's already been an extra-long and trying day. How about we order pizza, make some junk food, and pick out a couple of pay-per-view movies for tonight?"

"Sounds like the perfect date to me."

"I'll go call the pizza place," Kyle replies.

When he's out of the room, she leans in and whispers in my ear. "And later when we go to bed, we'll make sure we both get a happy ending today."

"I'll gladly give you all the happy endings you can stand. But are you sure you're up for it tonight?"

"Why not?" She smirks, using her list to make a point.

"Fair enough. I can hardly wait."

After watching the movies and finishing off all the pizza and junk food, we are all ready for bed. I'm nowhere near ready for sleep, but I'll follow Grace's lead. As hard as I tried to forget the news we received today long enough to enjoy spending time with my family, it was never far from my mind.

Every time she laughed at one of the stupid jokes in the

comedy, I memorized the sound. Burned every laugh line in her face into my brain.

When she cried during the sappy romance movie we watched, I saw the young girl I fell in love with in every tear that fell from her eyes. And I see my wife of eighteen years whom I love more than my own life. I watched her more than I did the TV, afraid to miss one second of our time together.

She closes and locks our bedroom door behind her, then leans against it with a come-hither expression on her beautiful face. "Time to get undressed for bed."

"You'll hear no argument from me. In fact, I'll even help you out of your clothes first."

"I'm waiting."

She only has to tell me once. Hesitation isn't an option, especially now. Especially when she's looking at me like she wants to devour me. Fuck if I don't want her to, but what I want most is to give her more than I ever have before. More than she can take in one night. Tonight is all about Grace and making her feel alive—and leaving no doubt that my heart and soul belong to her after I finish worshiping her body.

She stays rooted in her spot when I set my sights on her and move toward her. Her breathing hitches, and her skin flushes with excitement. I peel her clothes off with her standing up, savoring every brush of my fingers across her skin and pressing my lips against her softness as I move. Every inch of her is sheer perfection, beauty I'll never forget or take for granted again.

Her breathing increases with my every movement, her chest heaves with anticipation and desire. Just knowing how much she wants me fuels my libido exponentially. Kneeling in front of her, I gently push on her legs to widen them and give me room to work my magic. Her fingertips stroke my scalp as I begin my initial assault on her with slow, controlled flicks of my tongue. The strength of her grip on me increases in time with my intensity and pace.

"Oh God," she moans when I pick up her leg and put it over my shoulder.

She becomes louder when I drive deep inside her, lapping up her sweet nectar and rolling my tongue against her inner walls. When I thrust my fingers into her wetness, her knee buckles from the powerful sensations. I easily hold her up and slide her standing leg onto my shoulder, pushing her back against the door. The more eager my movements are, the farther her hips buck upward and expose her beautiful core to me.

When she screams my name and her body quivers from her release, I slow my ministrations and ease her legs to the floor. Then I scoop her up in my arms and move her to the bed where I can finish my mission to rock her world.

I'll take my time and make this last all night. Reconnecting with Grace heals the brokenness inside me.

CHAPTER 16

Grace

Over the last few days, Blake and Kyle have been busy working on their Why Not lists. Since I refused to let them see mine until they've finished their own, they won't let me see theirs either. They claim if they have something cool on their list, I'll try to steal it and make it my own. I can't help but laugh at them even though they've ganged up against me and given me the exact same answers.

Whatever they list is fine by me, in all honesty. The consideration that goes into the items on their lists—the meaning behind those items—is what matters to me. Because this exercise is about more than squeezing in as many activities as we can before my time is up. Thinking about everything they want to do and achieve while *they* have time will keep them going long after I'm gone. They'll finish seeing their hopes and dreams through to fruition—for me, for each other, and for themselves. They'll have something to look forward to doing together, accomplishments they can be proud of achieving.

"I have to go out for a while. Will you be okay here without me?" Blake moves up behind me and wraps his arms around me.

Memories of last night immediately flood my mind the moment he touches me. Every night since my diagnosis, he has made love to me in ways that have lifted me to the stars and kept me there for hours. I've seen fireworks go off behind my eyelids and thought the heat from my body would set the bed on fire. Each night has been better than the last, to the point I can't wait to go to bed at night just to experience the thrill only he can give me.

"I'll be fine. Where are you going?"

"I can't tell you—it's a surprise. But if you need me for anything at all, call me and I'll come rushing home."

Before he can leave, I raise up on my toes and press my lips to his then wrap my arms around him in a warm embrace. He hesitates for a second, unsure of what's on my mind, then his arms encircle my waist.

"What's going on in that beautiful brain of yours?"

"Just a promise I made to myself," I reply.

While I watch Blake pull out of our driveway, my phone rings. I'm not surprised to see Leigh's name flash up on the screen.

"Hey, Leigh, what's up?"

"Oh, I don't know. Let me think. Maybe that my best friend just suddenly took off work without a word, is on medical leave, and hasn't called me to tell me what the hell is going on. I'm on my way to your house right now. Don't you dare leave."

"I'm here," I chuckle. "Come on over, and I'll fill you in."

With a fresh pot of coffee set to brew, I don't have to wait long before Leigh walks through the door. "Let's hear it—and no holding back. I know you better than you know yourself, so I'll know if you're keeping secrets from me." Then she stops and finally looks at me. "Holy shit. You're gorgeous even when you're bald. Do you know how hideous I would be?"

I can't help but laugh. This is what my best friend does for me

—she understands my crazy and meets it with her own. "Thank you. And no secrets, Leigh. I'll tell you every detail."

We take a seat with our full coffee cups in hand, and I recount everything that's happened since the day I left the hospital without an explanation. When I finish talking, I realize neither of us has taken the first sip, and our coffee is already cold. So much has happened in such a short time. So much that has changed my entire life and everything I thought I knew about it.

"Shit, Grace," Leigh says and wipes tears from her eyes before they fall to her cheeks. She looks around the kitchen, avoiding eye contact with me until she's more composed. "I was not expecting to hear this news at all."

"Me either. I mean, I knew it was a possibility later, but I just didn't think it would happen as soon as I was diagnosed. Leigh, Blake and Kyle will need your help when I'm gone. I'm keeping my life insurance through the hospital, so you may have to guide them through the process when it comes time."

"Grace, dammit. Don't talk like that." Leigh stands abruptly and stomps over to the microwave to heat her coffee. And avoid me.

"Leigh, you know as well as I do how life can turn on a dime. I can't leave my family in the lurch if I get more bad news next month or the next."

"How often are your scans?" she asks. Her back is to me, but her soft tone reflects she knows I'm right.

"Every three months, unless I develop new symptoms before then."

"So we're living from scan to scan, holding our breath until we know you're stable." She drops her chin to her chest and covers her mouth with her hand. Tears fill my eyes because I know my best friend is hurting as badly as I am.

"Leigh, you can cry. It doesn't mean you're weak," I say as I place my hand on her back.

The contact seems to be all it takes, because her sobs break free and her chest heaves with her pent-up angst. She turns and wraps me in her arms, resting her forehead on my shoulder. I pat her back and start to tell her everything will be okay, but I stop myself before the words come out.

"I'm okay for now, Leigh. We still have time together. And in the next few years, maybe new treatments will be available or researchers will have a breakthrough. I'm not giving up hope yet, and neither are you."

"You're right. I know you are. But I'm just so heartbroken—for you, Kyle, and even Blake. And for myself. Have you told your parents yet?"

"No, I actually haven't told them anything. I wasn't about to tell them before I told Blake and Kyle, and especially not on Christmas Eve after not seeing them for so long. But I know I have to tell them now. I just hate to show up with a bald head and shock them."

"Honey, they'll be shocked and upset whether you have a head full of hair or not. If it makes you feel better, I'll take you shopping, and we'll find all the best scarves and hats for you to wear. You'll need them to keep your head warm anyway."

"So do Blake and Kyle. We can find them a few extra hats, too."

"Why do they need them?"

"They shaved their heads bald so I wouldn't be the only one people stare at when we go out."

"That was Blake's idea, wasn't it?"

I nod and give her a small smile.

"Damn him. He's making it impossible for me to stay mad at him."

"Life is too short to stay mad. Or unhappy. Or anything else you don't want to be."

I grab my beanie knit hat and matching scarf from my room, and Leigh and I head out for a few hours of retail therapy and girlfriend time. When we've finished our rounds at the mall, I have several bags of hats, scarves, and other types of head coverings that I can't even remember the names of for all of us. Leigh drops me off with a kiss on the cheek and a demand for a standing weekly girls-only date so she's not left out of the loop.

When I walk inside, I find Blake pacing back and forth across the length of the den, so lost in his own thoughts he didn't even hear me come in.

~

Blake

"PENNY FOR YOUR THOUGHTS," Grace says from the doorway.

I stop mid-stride and lift my eyes to meet hers. She's wearing a cute little hat, puffy on top with a big bow on the side, and she's eyeing me from under the brim. She still takes my breath away with her beauty—inside and out.

"I'm thinking I love you. And I couldn't wait for you to get home. And I'm very curious as to how you're going to react. I hope you love it, but you can tell me if you hate the idea." Then I notice all the shopping bags hanging on her arm and rush to take them from her.

"I'm all ears. What do you have in mind?" She moves into the room as I drop the armload of bags onto the couch.

"I'll show you." I roll up the sleeve of my shirt and expose the colorful tattoo I had inked while she was out shopping. Her mouth drops open, and her eyes grow wider. "Do you know what it means?"

She shakes her head. "Only the line underneath. 'Until the end of time.' What are these symbols? The one in the middle looks like a heartbeat on a heart monitor strip. The watercolor shades behind the symbols are gorgeous, Blake. Those colors really make the shapes jump off your arm."

The watercolors give the symbols their shape and definition. The black outline of each symbol is connected to the next, showing the continuous cord that binds them. "The first one is a cross, that stands for faith. In my case, it also represents Grace. You, Grace. The second one is the heartbeat symbol from an EKG strip, it means hope. The last one is an open heart, and it means love. Faith, hope, and love for everyone else. *Grace*, hope, and love for me. Until the end of time."

"Blake, I can't believe you got a tattoo. You've never wanted one before."

"I didn't, and I really can't have visible ones because of my job. But I'll wear this one like my badge of honor." I hesitate, suddenly nervous to suggest my idea to my wife. "The tattoo artist said he can get you in this afternoon—in case you want to get a matching one."

I hold my breath, unsure of how she'll react. I'm not even sure she wants something permanently inked on her body that also connects her to me. I'm positive I don't deserve it if she does. But I'll never regret my constant reminder. I'll never lose the love of my life like I did before. She's forever in my heart, on my mind, and in my soul. This colorful ink is to let the rest of the world know who owns me.

"You had me tattooed on your body? Permanently?" She sounds so shocked, so amazed, so pleased.

"I did. It was on my Why Not list, almost at the top. So I thought, why not get it done today? No time like the present, right?"

"Absolutely. You made an appointment for me?"

"Not exactly. I wasn't sure if you'd want to be saddled with a permanent reminder of me. But I may have asked him about getting you in today if you decided you wanted one too."

"I do want it, Blake. I'd love to have one just like yours. Faith, hope, and love—that's what keeps me going."

"Can you get a tattoo while you're on chemotherapy drugs?"

"Technically, I'm supposed to wait because of the chance of infection. But I'm early in my regimen, and I'm a nurse, so I'll take good care of it. I know others who have broken the rules and gotten one."

"We can wait. I don't want your arm to get infected and cause problems."

"Everything has risks, Blake. I'm willing to accept the risk, especially since I've only had two treatments. I'll have to be extra-careful soon enough. Let's have some fun now."

Although I'm reluctant, Grace is insistent and threatens to drive herself if I don't take her. I love her spirit and how she laughs in death's face. But now I'll watch her even closer to make sure she stays as healthy as possible for as long as possible. She's out of the car and nearly skipping toward the door before I can turn off the car and get out.

"Hey, Gary. I'm back with my wife, after all. She wants the same design." I walk up and shake his hand, having already explained her medical condition and what this couple's session means to us.

"You must be Grace. This guy wouldn't shut up about you. You're even prettier than he described. I'm thinking you should dump this guy and run away with me." Gary is an older man with the personality of someone who never meets a stranger. Apparently, he's also a huge flirt and wants to steal my wife away from me.

"Don't make me have to kill you with your own tattoo gun, Gary."

"That's cold, man." Gary shakes his head with a chuckle. "Have a seat, pretty lady, and show me where you want me to caress your skin with my ink."

Grace giggles and slides into the chair. She holds out her left arm, the opposite side from where her breast cancer is. "Put it in the same spot as Blake's so we'll match when we hold hands. His right to my left."

"I can add my name in here if you want." Gary winks at her then cuts his teasing eyes over to me.

"Maybe next time. Let me think about where I'd want it," Grace replies.

I think Gary's face actually just turned red.

An hour and a half later, Grace and I pull into our driveway, and she's still staring at her new adornment. Gary gave us strict instructions for keeping it clean and dry, but I know Grace will double the efforts to avoid any problems.

"I love this, Blake. After all our years together, I never thought we'd do something so impulsive as getting matching tattoos. But it feels right, doesn't it?"

"Yes, it does. We should've done this a long time ago. No more waiting. No more regrets. Right, babe?

"That's exactly right. Thank you for suggesting this. It's perfect, and it'll feel good marking that off the list, won't it?"

"Absolutely. There are a few more things I want to mark off my list soon. I'm working on them, so get ready to move fast."

"I'm all yours, and I'm ready to move at lightning speed."

CHAPTER 17

Grace

"We're with you, babe." Blake squeezes my hand then lifts it to his lips to kiss along my knuckles. "We'll help you."

I've avoided this unpleasant task for as long as I can, and there's no way another day can go by with it left undone. Blake, Kyle, and I are headed to my parents' house to break the news to them. Last night was terrible when we told Blake's parents, and after we left their house, I was in no shape to talk to my mom and dad. All the years his parents have been by my side, they've viewed me as one of their own kids.

Unloading this burden on my family and friends is almost as bad as getting the diagnosis itself. No one knows what to say when they're given life-altering news. I don't know what to say in response to their stunned silence or their shocked concern. We humans are all terrible at consoling each other under such unexpected circumstances.

Dad meets us at the door with hugs and a smile, and I immediately feel guilty for knowing I'm about to take that bright smile away from him. "Grace, I didn't know you were coming over. I'm so glad to see you."

"It's good to see you too, Daddy. Is Mom home?"

"Yes, she's in the living room. We were just watching a little TV. Come on it."

"I could really get used to these visits from my favorite people in the world." Mom greets us at the door to the living room in much the same way Dad did. Surprised but happy to see us and eager for us to sit and talk to them. She beams as she hugs each of us, then invites us to make ourselves at home.

I notice how she keeps staring at Kyle. She looks away, but her line of sight inevitably moves back to him within a few seconds. A forlorn expression crosses her face, and she looks down at the floor.

"What's on your mind, Mom?"

"I was just thinking about how much Kyle looks like you when you were his age. Then I realized you were the same age he is now when you last lived at home. Time is just flying by, and I don't have a clue where it has gone."

Blake and I exchange knowing glances. "I know exactly what you mean. That's actually why we're here. I have some bad news I need to share with you both."

Nothing about this discussion is easy—not for my parents, my husband, my son, or me. But when I lift the hat from my head, Blake and Kyle follow suit.

I tell them everything I know about my diagnosis, prognosis, and treatment plan. From the time I entered nursing school, we were taught to be blunt so there were no misunderstandings. If our patient died, we said he died. He didn't pass away. He's not no longer with us. He's dead. The direct answer can sting at times, but having a distraught family member misunderstand the status of their loved one is worse. That technique was ingrained in me fifteen years ago when I was in nursing school, and tonight is no exception.

They have to understand how serious this is and how quickly my status could change in the future.

As I expected, Mom starts crying almost immediately. But I never expected what follows. Overcome with grief and distraught, she slides off the couch and onto the floor before burying her face in the crook of her arm. Her wails fill the room, not at all diminished by her position. Her whole body shakes with her cries. My dad, wiping tears from her face with one hand, wraps his other arm around her and does his best to console her.

"Gretchen, you need to pull yourself together. Grace needs us to be strong for her now."

Mom nods her head. "You're right. I'm sorry, I don't mean to make any of this about me. It's not at all. Grace, I wish I could take this from you. If it meant you were cured, I'd take it without a second thought."

"We both would," Dad says. "What can we do to help? Whatever you need is yours."

"There's nothing I need you to do right now, except keep your family close. *All* of your family. Whatever the future brings, Blake and Kyle will need your support and love."

Mom pulls herself up off the floor with Dad's help and moves on shaky legs to sit beside Blake. She wraps her hand around his and meets his questioning gaze. "Blake, I've been so wrong about you for so long, and I'm so sorry for how we treated you. Grace was so young and so in love with you, but I was convinced she was throwing her life away. Matt and I thought we were doing what was best for her, that tough love would bring her back to us. We regret the years apart, but I've never been so glad to be wrong about someone. You obviously still love each other as much today as you did back then. Probably even more now. Thank you for taking such good care of our daughter, especially when we weren't there to care for her."

"Thank you for saying that, Gretchen. It means a lot to me." Blake wraps his arm around her shoulders and pulls her into him for a friendly hug. Instead, she releases his hand and throws her arms around him and squeezes tightly.

She sits back, drying her wet face with her hands, and releases a deep sigh. "What do we do now?"

"We enjoy the rest of the evening together," I say. "Like you said, time is flying by, and we can't stop it. So we'll just make the best of it instead."

After forty-five minutes of torture from looking through every picture taken of me from infancy until I left home, Dad, Blake, and Kyle retreat to the man cave and leave Mom and me alone to finish our trip down memory lane. As they walk past, Blake leans down and kisses me, but I can sense his mood is off. He's apprehensive about something, though nothing has happened tonight to throw him off-kilter.

My eyes crinkle at the corners, and my brows draw downward slightly, silently questioning him. He answers with a half smile and a slight shake of his head, telling me not to worry about it. It's amazing how well I can read him and know something's bothering him now—again. I lost that sixth sense about him for a while, when we were disconnected and just drifting through life. Now that we've made a more focused effort to pay attention to each other, so many signs are right before my eyes.

"Grace, I just don't understand," Mom says, pulling me from my thoughts.

"Understand what, Mom?"

"We don't have a family history of breast cancer. I don't know one other person in our entire family who has ever faced this. How can this be? Have you had a second opinion?" She wipes tears from the corners of her eyes and inhales deeply, trying to stave off the emotions overtaking her again.

"My diagnosis has been confirmed, Mom. I don't need another opinion. And, as far as family history, that's only one factor. No one has a family history of it until someone in the family has it. There's a lady I see when I go for chemo who was only thirty-one when she was first diagnosed. Her name is April, and she's my age now. She's so sweet, Mom. She ran four miles a day, ate a healthy diet, and had no family history. She had surgery a few years ago, they removed all of the tumor, and she had clear margins—but it still returned. The cancer metastasized to her bones, and she's undergoing treatment to keep her tumors stabilized. This disease can literally happen to anyone, without warning and without cause."

"I suppose I have to accept this is really happening, then." She sounds defeated, as if her dreams were ripped from her fingers and linger just outside of her reach. "You don't seem to be as affected by it as I am. I guess that makes me keep thinking there's a chance the doctor was wrong."

"We all have to accept this is happening, Mom, but we each have to do it in our own way. It's okay to be sad, mad, hopeless. It's even okay to be in denial. I've had more time to adjust to the initial diagnosis than you have. This new turn wasn't expected, and I'm cycling through all the stages of grief every hour myself. I may seem okay right now, but I'm not always this calm. Trust me."

"I need a drink. What can I get you?"

"Just some water, please. My chemo cocktail doesn't mix well with alcohol."

"You'll have to teach me all about this—the medications, the interactions, the side effects. I want to understand so I'll know when and how I can help you."

A fact I haven't wanted to admit to pops into my mind. We all need our mother, no matter how old we are. *Please, God. I want to be there for Kyle when he needs me.*

"Grace, Blake works for a pharmaceutical company. Can't he find out if they have some miracle in a pill they're working on and get you into the trials?"

"The process doesn't quite work like that, Mom. But don't think he hasn't made call after call to verify that for himself. As long as my proven combination works, my doctor wouldn't chance changing my medications. What if I stopped this course and started another one, only to find out it doesn't work? That would allow the cancer to grow uninhibited. I'll only do clinical trials as a last-resort treatment."

Her panic-stricken face is the only reply I need to know she understands what I'm saying.

"Now, if there's a medication trial that would be used in conjunction with my current regimen, I would do that—if it was shown to reduce or eliminate the tumors, for example."

"Let's hope and pray for a powerful breakthrough along those lines, then."

On the ride home, I reflect on the night with my parents. Part of me, a big part of me, wishes we'd had eighteen years of this so that Kyle would've had both sets of grandparents while growing up. So that Blake and I would've had more support and felt less alone. But I realize I can't keep living in wishes and what-ifs. Living in the now is more than enough to manage, and this life is what we have now.

"You three men disappeared for a while. What were you up to in the man cave?"

"Mom, what happens in the man cave stays in the man cave. At least until we're ready to reveal our secrets."

I laugh, because I can't help but feel amused by my son's continued antics. He hasn't changed toward me, he isn't treating me with kid gloves, and I love that. "Oh yeah, little boy? I'm still your mother—I can beat it out of you."

"That's child abuse, you know. I *will* report you to the authorities."

Now, I'm really laughing. "Yes, you do that. Let's go stand before a judge. We'll let him see how much bigger you are than me, and he can decide who's being abused in this house."

Kyle laughs along with me, playful as ever. "We could tell you, but then we'd have to kill you. I'm not old enough to be a murderer yet."

"There's a minimum age requirement?"

"Yeah, of course."

"What is it?"

"Not seventeen, almost eighteen. That's all I know."

"That's right." I nod, pretending I just remembered this important fact. "You do have a birthday coming up soon, don't you?"

"You wound me. How could you forget my birthday? I mean, I skipped an entire grade. I'm younger than everyone else in my class. My eighteenth birthday is a big deal, Mom. I'm so unappreciated in my own house."

Blake and I both laugh out loud at his pretend diva tirade.

"Yes, you've been so abused your entire life, son," Blake says.

"Can you say that again? Right into the microphone, please."

Laughing and joking with my little family feels so good. I've almost forgotten that my next treatment is tomorrow. I've almost forgotten I'll be three months into a five-month regimen. I've almost forgotten that after that fifth month, I'll have another scan to check the size of my tumors. I've almost forgotten that my life has changed in virtually every way I can possibly imagine.

But tonight, tonight is my now. This is where I live—in the moment.

"Hey, where'd you go? Did we lose you?" Blake asks and squeezes my hand in his.

"I have so many thoughts flying through my head at any given time, I'd swear I've recently developed ADD. But I'm right here where I'm meant to be, with you and Kyle. I'm not anywhere else, and there's nowhere else I'd rather be."

"Did you overdo it tonight? Was all this too much for you?"

"Not at all. Don't worry about me, Blake. I'll let you know if that ever happens."

"Good, because I'll take you home before your energy runs out. You have to save some up for me every night."

"You know, studies have shown that 96.3 percent of kids are traumatized by their parents' public displays of affection. You're traumatizing me beyond repair right now," Kyle chimes in from the back seat.

"I'm pretty sure you just made up those numbers and studies," I reply with a chuckle.

"I'm still 96.3 percent sure you're traumatizing me beyond repair. You can't talk about anything remotely related to...what you two were just talking about."

"Son, I think it's time you and I had *the talk*—the one about the birds and the bees," Blake says, his teasing smile lighting up his face.

"Oh God. You're killing me. This is cruel and unusual punishment. You're violating my rights. Stop the car! I'll walk home."

Our laughter fills the car for the rest of the ride home—at Kyle's expense—while he pretends to stew in the back seat. I catch him smiling to himself when he turns his head, trying to hide his amusement, though.

These moments are what matter.

The small things in life *are* the big things.

CHAPTER 18

Blake

race had her third chemotherapy treatment earlier this week. She said the past two weren't too bad. She felt tired for a couple of days then seemed to bounce back fairly quickly. She doesn't seem to be recovering too easily after this week's round, driving my concern for her through the roof. I'm leaning against the counter, drinking a cup of coffee and watching her intently for any sign of an underlying problem.

"Stop staring at me. You're starting to freak me out," she says without looking up from her tablet.

"How do you know I'm staring at you? You're busy reading."

"I can feel your eyes on me. You're distracting me from my book."

"Are you blushing from me watching you or from what you're reading? You know, I can do more for you than those imaginary men in your romance books can."

A smile covers her face despite her attempt to remain unamused by my intrusion into her reading time. "That is very true. You do."

"How can I entice you to put that book down and talk to me instead?"

"Hmm." She pretends to think about her reply. "A back massage might persuade me."

"That's a deal I won't pass up." I move up behind her chair at the table and slide my hands under her sweater. The second I touch her skin, I know I was right to worry about her. "Grace, you're burning up. Have you checked your temperature?"

"No," she replies but avoids making eye contact with me.

"Nurses make the worst patients," I mumble and head to the medicine cabinet to get the thermometer. When it shows she has a fever of 102 degrees, my full protective mode kicks into overdrive. "Call your oncologist and tell him. I'll go pack an overnight bag for the hospital stay I know is coming."

"This is exactly why I didn't tell you."

"You asked for a back rub. How did you think I wouldn't feel how hot you are?"

"I didn't expect you to try to take my sweater off. I thought you'd just massage through it."

"As high as your fever is, I still would've felt it. Call the doctor. Now."

I take the stairs two at a time, rush into the bedroom, and start throwing the items we'll need into an overnight bag. She's on chemo, her immune system is compromised, and she's running a fever. I won't lose her to a common cold because she's too stubborn to follow the rules. And it has to be a regular cold, because I can't accept the alternative reasons that would explain why she'd be running a fever now.

She's just hanging up with the doctor's office when I rejoin her in the kitchen. "Well, what did they say?"

"Go to the ER. Tell them I'm on chemo and running a fever so they don't dismiss me as just having a common cold. He'll meet us there. Bring an overnight bag just in case." She recites the instructions without emotion, but I can read between the lines. I can read her as well as she can read the book that held her attention so raptly.

She's scared, like I am.

I wrap my arms around her from behind and rest my chin on her shoulder. "Babe, what other symptoms are you hiding from me?"

She sighs. "Fatigue. My throat is a little sore. Fever. Headache. Dry cough. Body aches."

"Sounds like the flu to me, babe. Let's go get you tested, maybe hook you up with some IV fluids to flush this out of you, and hopefully, we'll be on our way back home tomorrow morning."

"What about Kyle?"

"If it takes that long, I'll call him when he gets out of school and explain. Or I'll be here to pick him up and bring him back to the hospital with me. Either way, I'll take care of him, and I'll take care of you."

"I'm scared, Blake." She turns and buries her face in my chest, her fingers gripping the front of my shirt.

This is the first time she's shown any real fear around me, the first time she's been vulnerable at all about her condition. Staying positive about the future is easier when she's strong and upbeat every day. Seeing her fear take over her normal optimistic nature stuns me silent for a moment while I try to think of the right thing to say.

"Grace, I won't lie to you. Everything about this disease scares me. We can only take this one day at a time. No matter what happens, I'll be right here beside you. When you're weak, I'll be your strength. When you're in a dark place, I'll be your light. I'll never leave you, babe. I love you, until the end of time."

"Do you remember why we started saying that to each other?"

Like a knife driven deep into my chest, the stabbing pain of that time returns to remind me. As if I could ever forget.

"The whole world against us. Everyone told us we wouldn't last, we were too young, we had our whole lives ahead of us, we shouldn't have the baby, we should take a break from each other. Everywhere we turned, it seemed someone urged us to give up on everything we knew we wanted.

"If memory serves, it was after one particularly nasty fight with your parents, we sat in my car, and I held you while you cried. They said I'd leave you to raise our baby on your own, and that I was just using you to get what I wanted then I'd move on to the next girl in line. You asked me how I was so sure that would never happen. I told you all I needed was your love until the end of time. If you could promise me that, I could live without everyone else."

She doesn't respond, but she doesn't move either. With my arms wrapped around her, I can feel her body temperature, and the high fever concerns me. I have to get her to the hospital for immediate treatment. We can't let anything get out of control— it'll be too hard to get her health back in line if we do. She's worried the fever and other symptoms are a sign that her tumors are growing or have already spread elsewhere. We've had enough bad news to last us a lifetime; we don't need more. But we can't avoid the symptoms altogether either.

"Let's go, babe. You feel even hotter now than you did a few minutes ago. We'll get through this together, no matter what is thrown at us. But I still say you caught the flu from someone, and your body just can't fight it off because of the chemo. That's my official diagnosis."

"All right, let's go, then. I'm holding you to that diagnosis, though."

She maintains a tight grip on my hand during the entire ride to the ER. Her fears roll off of her and crash into me like tidal waves, but I maintain my composure. She's worked up enough for both of us, and it's my turn to be her strength.

Dr. Evers is already in the ER when we arrive, so thankfully, he helps us bypass the usual triage process and takes Grace straight back. Although, Grace knows all the nurses in this department since the ER and ICU share nurses in shortages and emergency situations, so they probably would've sent her straight back anyway.

"We'll test for the flu first because I agree these symptoms are classic and would easily explain your fever. But since I don't leave anything to chance, we'll also run a few more lab tests and go from there. Plan on spending a night or two. We'll get your IV started to push fluids into you. If you test positive for the flu, we'll start you on antiviral medicines to help lessen the duration," Dr. Evers says.

He leaves the room to write out his orders and schedule the tests, and a nurse Grace is friends with walks in with a hospital gown and kit to start her IV, followed by a lab tech with a throat swab. After the flu test swab is done, I help Grace change clothes and get comfortable in the bed.

Then the nurse spies the new tattoo on her inner arm.

"When did you get that?" Patti asks, placing her hand on her hip and piercing Grace with a knowing stare.

"Umm…recently," Grace admits.

"Grace Hardy. You know you shouldn't get tattoos while you're on chemo. The risk of infection is too high."

"I know, but it's not infected. It's already healed, so that's not what's causing these symptoms."

Patti cuts her eyes at me. "You let her do this?"

"Let her? Like I could stop her from doing something she wants to do."

Then Patti spots the matching tattoo on my arm. "You two got matching ink. While she's on chemo. Are you both crazy?"

"Nurses make the worst patients. You know that," Grace quips.

Patti laughs, not denying the fact, and gets Grace's IV going. "We'll get you well, hon. I'll be back when we get some test results and I know which way your treatment will go, but you call me if you need anything at all until then."

"Thanks, Patti."

When we're alone again, Grace looks up at me. "I know you need to work today. I'm okay here alone if you need to leave. It'll be a while before we know anything."

"I'm not going anywhere. I took the day off, so I'm all yours."

Twenty minutes later, Patti comes back into the room. "Grace, your flu test is positive. We're going to start you on the antiviral meds now. It won't make you feel better right away, but it should help you get over it faster. Dr. Evers still wants to do a few other tests while you're here, though. You're being admitted, so we'll transfer you up to a regular room in a few minutes."

"If it's just the flu, why is he running other tests? Just treat me and let me go home."

"You'll find Dr. Evers errs on the side of caution with his patients—always. Try not to worry about anything just yet."

Easier said than done, Patti.

∾

Grace

AFTER TWO NIGHTS of IV hydration, medications, and Blake babying me with ice chips and cold compresses, I woke up this morning feeling better than I have in a long time. My fever spiked again after I was admitted, and that scared me. I mean, it really scared me. Dr. Evers hadn't planned to do a new scan at this time to see if my tumors had grown or had spread anywhere else, but I strongly insisted.

Okay, in all honesty, my hysterics when my fever was still high yesterday scared Brent, and he relented to pacify me.

Now that I know my symptoms are truly from the flu and I already feel better today than I did yesterday, I'm able to rest easy again. Just having that verification in my back pocket takes a huge weight off my shoulders and clears my hazy vision. When I was sure the end was nearer than I originally thought, I couldn't focus on anything else other than how much of my family's lives I'd miss.

Now that I can see the big picture of my life again, I'm even more determined to check items off my Why Not list every day.

"Blake?" He's asleep beside me, squeezed into this small hospital bed. With his head lying on my chest, I have free access to run my fingers over his neck and back. "Blake, honey?"

"Hmm?" He doesn't move away from me—he tightens his arm around me.

"I need three things."

"What do you need?"

"First, I need you to wake up." I chuckle and lovingly stroke his cheek with my fingertips.

"I'm awake. Sort of."

"Second, I really need to pee. My IV is still running wide open."

"And third?"

"I need you to bring my Why Not list from home if Dr. Evers decides to keep me another day."

That gets his attention.

He lifts his head and grins. "That means I actually get to see it. How about I help you to the bathroom then I'll rush home and grab it for you?"

"How about you help me to the bathroom then we'll see what the doctor says when he comes in?"

Blake slides up in the bed and snuggles into the crook of my neck. "Go ahead and tell me where it is, just in case."

He's so obvious, but then, he's not actually trying to be sly. We both know he has wanted to see my list since the day I asked him and Kyle to make their own. The only reason I haven't shown him is because I don't want him so focused on working through my list that we never check items off his. Then it hits me—we want the same thing. We both want to see the other happy and fulfilled.

"It's in the top drawer of my nightstand, in my black leather ARC notebook."

He quickly raises up on his elbow and gives me the most bewildered look. "Are you serious?"

"Yes, I'm serious. Why wouldn't I be?"

"Does this mean I can finally see it?"

"Absolutely. Then you can help me pick which one of mine— and yours—we're going to check off today. I don't want to wait any longer to do all the things on our minds and in our hearts."

"I want you to know it means a lot to me that you're sharing your thoughts and dreams with me, Grace. I'll bring my list back with me too, and you can go through every line. Babe, I can't wait to start living the rest of my life with you."

Blake helps me to the bathroom, then hangs around long enough to help me shower before he leaves. When my morning nurse comes in for one of her rounds, she eyes me suspiciously.

"You took a shower again this morning, didn't you?"

"I did. I can't stand not having one first thing when I wake."

"And your IV?"

I shrug. "I'm an ICU nurse. I know how to unhook it and secure it long enough to bathe."

She shakes her head, knowing she can't stop me, and continues checking my vitals. "Your fever is below 100 degrees. That's a good sign."

"It's still early, though. It's usually higher in the afternoons than it is first thing in the morning. Think Dr. Evers will let me go home today anyway?"

"If it stays down by the time he makes rounds, he may discharge you. I will warn you, he normally waits until there's no sign of fever at all, though. If he does let you go, he'll expect you to keep a close watch on it and come straight back if it spikes again."

I can handle that. Now that I know which medicines I'm allowed take for my flu symptoms, I'll be much more able to treat it in the comfort of my own home. Blake and Kyle will also be there to make sure I don't get away with anything.

My cell phone rings, and I smile when I see Blake's face fill my screen. "Hello. Are you already home and reading my Why Not list?"

"I am—and you have some great ideas on here. I can't wait to cross a lot of these off your list." His chuckle warms my heart, because I know he's picturing us together with every single item. "Are you okay there alone for a little while? I had an urgent voice-mail from Rob about one of my large specialty doctor groups. They need me on a conference call this morning. But if you need me there with you, I can take the call on my cell."

"I'll be just fine. Don't worry about me. My fever is already coming down. I hope Dr. Evers sends me home today. Take your time and handle your doctors' questions and concerns. I'm not going anywhere. Maybe by the time you're finished working, I'll be all set to come home."

"That would be the best news. I'll call you as soon as this meeting is over. I love you, babe. Get plenty of rest, and I'll talk to you soon."

We disconnect, and I lean my head back on the pillow. My heart finally feels like it's starting to mend. The stitches we've put in place over time are beginning to close the gaping wound that was once there. For the first time in a very long while, I feel hope blossoming in my chest. Despite my cancer. Despite my prognosis. Despite what's happened between us in the past.

My life, my heart, and my soul will be full of love and happiness.

CHAPTER 19

Grace

"How's my favorite patient today?" Brent asks as he breezes into my room midafternoon after already keeping me in the hospital for two nights.

"You're only saying that because you made me stay an extra night. I was ready to go home yesterday. And now you show up late in the day instead of first thing in the morning."

"No, you weren't ready to go home before today. You still had a fever yesterday, and your immune system is compromised enough as it is. You needed the fluids and meds to help flush the flu out of your system. Looks like your fever has stayed below 100 degrees all day today. That's a good sign. How do you feel otherwise?"

"Much better. Good enough to go home today. Right now."

"Okay, Grace. I'll start your discharge papers. Call your husband and let him know he can take you home in about an hour."

"Thank God. I miss my bed so much."

"But if you have any change in temperature, you call me immediately," Brent demands with a pointed look.

"Yes, Dr. Evers. I promise I will take good care of myself. While I love working here, I don't like sleeping here at all."

When Brent leaves my room, I immediately call Blake to give him the good news. But his tone when he answers concerns me.

"Hey, babe. Sorry I'm not back yet. One call led to another, and now everything just feels like a huge clusterfuck. Is everything all right?"

"I'm better than all right. Brent just said I can go home today. He said you can pick me up in about an hour. Does that work for you?"

"Of course it does. For you, I'll make it work."

"Want to tell me what's going on at work?"

"Sales are down in my territory. That means my work ethic is being questioned, my commitment to my doctors, my allegiance to the company. Everything. There's fierce competition in pharmaceuticals, and getting doctors to switch brand-name drugs they're used to prescribing is hard sometimes."

I think about all the years Blake has worked in a job he doesn't love but has been successful at nonetheless. For possibly the first time ever, I consider what it would be like to spend the majority of my life being trapped in a position that sustained my family's way of life, but left me completely unfulfilled. That's where Blake has been for far too long—stuck in that disappointing rut between dreams and reality.

"What can I do to help?"

"You're already doing it, babe. You're coming home. Let me finish these couple of emails I'm working on, then I'll be on my way."

"I'm so ready. Don't forget about me. I'll see you soon."

"Not a chance. I'll fly like the wind. I love you, babe."

We hang up, and I impatiently begin preparing myself for discharge as much as I can. If the nurse on duty hadn't taken all the medical supplies I tried to pilfer, I could remove my own IV and save her the trouble. And save myself some time. Instead, I stop the pump and disconnect the line so I can at least change into my street clothes. With everything packed, I wait on pins and needles for my discharge. I'm so ready to get home and get started on our lists, even the TV can't hold my interest.

When my nurse finally enters my room, she stops and looks at me, fully dressed, and shakes her head. "You know, I get the feeling you're ready to skip out on me."

"Leslie, I love you, but I don't want to see your face while I'm on this side of the door ever again."

We both laugh, and she goes through her required spiel of making sure I understand the discharge orders. When she reaches the page for my responsible party and driver to sign, I explain Blake is on his way back.

"You know I can't discharge you without knowing you have a ride. Dr. Evers will have my head."

"Take me downstairs, and we'll wait for him. He's already on his way, I promise you. He can sign the papers while I jump in the car and lock the door."

"You're just getting over a high fever. I can't let you sit outside until he gets here, Grace."

"Fine. I'll text him to meet us at the ER. We can sit inside and watch for him through the ambulance bay doors. I'll stay warm, and we can stay out of their way behind the nurses' desk."

"Oh, all right. I could use a break anyway. Only for you, though."

"Ha. Only because you're eyeing that handsome intern down there. You're not fooling me, missy."

"Busted. Guilty as charged. Now let's go find Dr. Sexy and Single while we wait for your husband."

Leslie pushes the wheelchair, and I send a quick text to Blake, letting him know where to find me. When we arrive in the ER,

Leslie parks me behind the desk and takes the vacant seat beside me.

"Look, Grace, there he is."

I look up from my phone after checking to see if Blake has read my message yet and find the intern Leslie is fawning over. He is very good-looking, I must admit. But he's too young for my taste. He's closer to Leslie's age, young and not as experienced with how cruel life can be as I am. After he casually glances around the room, his gaze lands on Leslie first then on me sitting in a wheelchair in the emergency department.

His eyebrows draw down, unsure if we need help or if we're just visiting, so he strolls over to chat with us.

"Afternoon, ladies. Can I take your order?" Dr. Sexy-and-Single Terry Bowers asks.

"I'll have a signed hospital discharge with a side of my husband driving me home, please."

"Same for me, so I can rid of the worst patient I've ever had," Leslie jokes.

"The service in this hospital is terrible. Did anyone here actually go to medical school? Or did you all buy your degrees online?" I shoot back with a smile.

Terry sits on the desk beside Leslie, and the three of us laugh, shoot joking barbs back and forth at each other, and chat about my disease status since there are no secrets among medical friends. Leslie animatedly tells us about another one of her patients then abruptly stops talking.

"You are a horrible influence, Grace! I'm late getting back to work from my break. You're going to get me in trouble. Where is that husband of yours?"

My eyes shoot to the clock on the wall, and I'm alarmed at the amount of time that's passed while Leslie, Terry, and I have been chatting. Blake should've been here long ago. I jerk my phone out of my pocket and see no missed calls, so I quickly dial his number, but it rolls to voice mail after several rings.

A sinking feeling grows in the pit of my stomach where my heart has dropped. This is out of character for him—for the last few months anyway. Since we've reconnected. Since we've reconciled. Where is he?

"You can go on back up if you need to, Leslie. I'll keep her chart and get him to sign when he gets here. That'll give me an excuse to take a break and head up to your floor," Terry says.

"Sounds good to me. I'll see you soon, then. Grace, you take care, and call me if you need anything." Leslie gives me a quick kiss on the cheek and rushes back upstairs before her fellow nurses page her over the hospital intercom system.

Right now, I wish I had an intercom to reach Blake. Where could he be?

I try calling him again, but there's still no answer.

Then I hear the wail of ambulance sirens approaching from a distance. The times I've had to rotate to the ER to help with multiple injuries are ingrained in my mind. Approaching sirens alert everyone to get ready—something serious will burst through the ambulance bay doors any second. The teams are ready with their gowns and gloves on.

"What's going on? I didn't even hear the call come over the radio while we were talking."

"MVA. Several vehicles. Multiple injured and a couple of casualties."

MVA. Motor vehicle accident.

Dear God—Blake.

No!

I watch with bated breath as the first ambulance rolls into the covered bay, and the staff members rush to open the doors from the inside. The first patient is a middle-aged woman, her blond hair matted to her head with dark red blood. The paramedic keeping a quick pace at her side continues to squeeze the bag, forcing oxygen into her lungs while the emergency room doctor begins calling out orders to the team.

The second ambulance roars to a stop, and the paramedic driving rushes to the back to open the door and help pull the gurney out. Then I see him.

I'm not breathing.

I can't remember how to breathe.

The black hair.

The scruffy beard.

"Asystole... Intubated... CPR at ten minutes twenty-seven seconds now... Trauma to head, neck, and face... Multiple contusions, lacerations, and broken bones... Pupils dilated and fixed—no reaction to light or pain stimulus."

I hear the medical report in short bursts, but I'm unable to process all the words. As an ICU and ER nurse, I'm trained to deal with life-and-death situations. I've worked numerous codes under immense pressure, following the protocol and remaining level-headed but focused.

But at this moment, I can't remember a single step in the process.

The team works together to move him from the ambulance gurney, and I sit in stunned silence. A needle is jabbed deep into his chest and medicine is administered to try to restart his heart, but the monitor continues to show a flat line move across the screen. Inside my head, I'm screaming for help—*save him*—but no words will pass across my lips.

The ER doctor stops all efforts. "Let's call it. We've done all we can do. Time of death is 5:22 p.m."

Then I spring into action, jumping up from the wheelchair and running to the trauma bay where his lifeless body is still surrounded by medical personnel.

"Blake! No! Please, God, no! Don't do this to me! You have to save him—you can't give up on him! Blake!"

My face is wet with tears, and they drip off my cheeks onto the floor. The staff stares at me with understanding but sorrowful expressions, silently telling me they can't do anything else to save him. Somewhere in the back of my mind, I know too much time has passed without a heartbeat. I know he wouldn't want to live in a vegetative state even if they could restart his heart now. But it's *my* heart that won't accept it. I'll take him any way I can as long as he doesn't leave me now.

My knees give out, and I crumple to the floor in a heap of screams and wails, calling his name over and over.

"Grace? Are you hurt? My God, what happened? Talk to me, Grace!" Strong arms reach under my arms and lift me off the floor, pulling me up to my feet.

"Blake, don't leave me. Please don't leave me."

"I'm not going anywhere, babe. You're scaring me, though. What's wrong? What the hell is going on?"

The frantic voice behind me finally registers in my panicked brain, and I whirl around in his arms. Tears of grief and sorrow instantly turn to tears of relief and immense joy. I lift my hands, letting my fingers trace along the scruff of his beard up to his bald head. Then I remember—he shaved his black hair off for me.

"Blake? I thought—I thought... You're okay. You're not hurt."

He pulls me tighter to him when my emotions overtake me again, calmly assuring me that we're both fine, then pulls me out of the room so the staff can finish their job. I can't make my arms release him even long enough to look at him. Not even to walk out of the ER after he signs my discharge papers. Not as we cross the parking lot toward his car. He opens the passenger door for me to get in, but I'm still shaking too hard from that terrible experience.

"Grace, you have to talk to me, or I'm taking you back inside. You're scaring me."

My teeth are chattering, but not from the cold, making it hard to speak. "Y-you were l-late. I-I couldn't r-reach you. Th-then I s-saw that man d-die. I th-though I'd l-lost you."

He wraps his arms around me again, cocooning me in his protective embrace, and kisses the top of my head. "I'm so sorry, babe. Rob called me while I was on the way here, and I couldn't get off the phone to answer your call. I'm here with you—I'm fine. I'm not going anywhere. You can't get rid of me that easily."

He pulls back and forces me to look up at him. With the pads of his thumbs, he dries the tears from under my eyes. The pure love in his eyes is for me, and I feel it touch me all the way to my soul.

"I love you, Blake. I love you so much. I've been so afraid to tell you because I didn't want to be hurt again. But now I know I've been hurting both of us by not telling you every day how much you mean to me. I'm sorry for that. I've always loved you. I won't let another single day go by without letting you know how much I love and appreciate everything you do for me and Kyle."

He stares at me in disbelief for a second before he crushes his mouth to mine. Our kiss is instantly frantic and demanding. Passionate and needy. Consuming and possessive.

He's the first to end our kiss but keeps his forehead pressed against mine. "Babe, you've just made me the happiest man in the world, and you know I'd move heaven and earth for you. But you have to get in the car. You're just getting over the flu. I don't want you to get sick again."

"Blake, when I thought I'd lost you forever, I couldn't breathe. I didn't even want to live anymore. My whole world stopped when I thought you died right in front of me. That was the worst feeling I've ever experienced. My heart is still broken just thinking about it."

His smile can't hide the sorrow in his eyes. "I feel like that every time I think about your cancer."

He points to the seat, so I slide in and let him close the door. It's time I start recognizing all the little things he does simply to care for me.

CHAPTER 20

Blake

race and I hit a monumental turning point in our relationship after that day in the emergency room. Over the past month, we've been inseparable. Our relationship has never been better. I've never been happier—and that's what scares me the most. Without her, I'll never feel this exhilaration again. Every day has been better than the last, and the level of intimacy has only deepened.

She shares everything with me now. Her hopes. Her fears. Her dreams. Where she sees us in the coming years, after Kyle has graduated college and moved on with his own life. The places she wants to visit and the experiences she wants to have with me. Just the two of us enjoying our lives together as it was meant to be, and I know I'm as important to her as she is to me.

We're working through our Why Not lists together, crossing off multiple items at once when we can. It's amazing how many similar items we had on our lists. To think we could've started this years ago and been leaps and bounds ahead by today if we'd just talked and shared then. Why can't we start out old and become young?

Watch the sunrise and sunset in the same day. Check.

Get matching tattoos. Check.

Cuddle and stargaze in the middle of the night. Check.

"Blake, where are we going?" This only makes the sixty-third time she's asked since we got in the car.

"I'm certain I've already told you."

"You only said it was a surprise. You haven't told me anything."

"Oh, yeah. You're right. That's exactly what I said."

She laughs and adjusts her colorful scarf covering her head. All of our heads are still bald—hers, Kyle's, and mine. Our promise still holds true, though she has assured us she wouldn't mind if we decided to grow our hair back out. I can't go through the rigors of chemo with her, but I will do everything else I can to show my love and support.

Like today. Today is for her, even though she has no clue—not even the slightest idea—of what's in store. That's the best part, because I've found it is almost impossible to keep secrets from her now. I want to tell her everything. I want to share every aspect of my day with her. And when I arranged the series of events that will begin today, I was so excited there was only one person I wanted to tell. That one person is the only person I couldn't tell. So, technically, holding it in has been as hard on me as it has been for her not knowing what's in store.

But her reaction will be worth it. All the little details I've coordinated in secret will culminate into one grand design that she'll never forget. This is all about the end game.

"Blake, why are we pulling into my parents' driveway?"

"Is that where we are? How about that?"

She folds her arms over her chest and pretends to glare at me. Even though she finished her fourth treatment a few days ago, she feels better now than she has since this started. We know the cancer isn't gone, but we can live with it being stable. She can live with stable. One more treatment to go before she has another scan to check her tumors. More bloodwork to monitor. More waiting to confirm she'll live a while longer and determine what type of surgery she'll need.

Which is why we make every single day count now.

"I see you're going to force me to keep secrets from you now," she threatens.

"That depends on what the secret is and why you're keeping it."

She leans across the console and kisses my cheek. "Only the secrets that I plan to use for a surprise, my love."

"I approve of those secrets." I park the car and cup her cheek with my hand. With our lips pressed together, I take the time to inhale her scent and savor her taste before we go inside. "I don't know what I did to be so lucky to have you as my wife, but I thank God for you every day."

Gretchen steps out onto the front porch, her smile beaming wide from her barely contained excitement. I know how she feels —I'm having a hard time keeping it in myself.

"We're both blessed to have found each other, Blake. I wouldn't trade anything for my life with you."

"Your mom is waiting and watching. We'd better go inside now."

"Hello, sweetheart." Gretchen pulls Grace into a tight hug while flashing a big, toothy grin at me over her shoulder. "How do you feel today?"

She asks Grace this every day. Though Grace knows her mom is really asking if there's a change in her prognosis, Grace remains upbeat in her replies to help allay Gretchen's fears. Grace has said she'd be no different with her own child, so she can't expect her mother to stop asking. We've each learned to take it one day, one symptom at a time. Gretchen just needs more time to learn to deal with her worst fears.

"I'm good, Mom. No real side effects from my chemo past the

couple of days after the treatment. How are you?"

"Can't complain, but sometimes I still do." She laughs at her own joke then kisses my cheek hello. "Blake, you go on in and find Matt. I'm taking Grace with me."

"Yes, ma'am," I agree. I turn to Grace and withhold a chuckle at her puzzled expression. "I'll see you later, babe. I love you."

"I love you, honey. Even though you're keeping secrets from me."

"Good secrets. Only because I love you." I kiss her cheek and move inside, leaving her alone with Gretchen.

Matt is just inside the door, waiting for me in the foyer. "You ready for this?"

"More than ready. Let's get going."

∾

Grace

"Okay, Mom. You can tell me what's going on now."

Her responding smile lights up her face, but I know before she says a word, my attempt to get her on my side of this conspiracy failed. "You know, I would love to tell you, Grace. But I'm not going to because you deserve to be completely surprised. Come with me. We'll take my car."

"I know there's no point in asking where we're going."

"None at all."

We walk to her car and head toward the mall area. I'm not surprised by this route—all the restaurants and stores are in this part of town. She parks in front of one of the boutique stores across the parking lot from the main mall—the one store most people won't even walk into if their disposable income doesn't outweigh their discretionary income by a hefty percentage.

My parents definitely fall into that category.

"You've lost so much weight, most of your clothes are baggy on you now. I want to treat you to a few new outfits."

"That's really not necessary, Mom."

"It is for me, Grace. Please let me have this opportunity to spoil my only child."

"Fine. But the guilt trips will only work for so long," I reply with a smile.

"I'll take advantage of those guilt trips working on you for as long as I can get away with it. Time for a mother-daughter shopping excursion."

After an hour of trying on every outfit in the store in various sizes to make sure the chosen outfits fit me perfectly, we move on to the shoe store next door. Thank God I wore my comfortable Tieks that allow me to slip them on and off without a hitch. If I'd had to spend another hour tying and untying laces, I would've run screaming from the store and left Mom behind—guilt trip or not. After the lingerie store foray, I've had enough.

"Mom, seriously, you don't have to buy me any more clothes. The trunk is full as it is. I'll never be able to wear all the outfits you've already made me pick out. I'm in scrubs most of the time anyway."

"Have you returned to work? I thought you were out on long-term disability now."

"I am—but I hope to return to work one day soon. I only have one more chemotherapy treatment."

What I can't say aloud is after my next treatment, we'll assess my condition again and decide what type of surgery I need. Lumpectomy or mastectomy. Either way, I'll eventually need reconstructive surgery down the road. Cancer steals so much time and energy. Time that I could spend doing so many other things I actually want to do.

"I've lost out on getting to spoil you all these years, Grace. This is fun for me—I enjoy buying nice things for you. The things I know you'd never buy for yourself because you put everyone else in your life ahead of yourself. Are you too tired to keep going? Have I pushed you too far?"

"No, I'm okay, Mom. Where else did you want to go?"

"Just one more place. But since I know your size, I can run in and grab something, and you can wait in the car. I know exactly what I want for your surprise."

"Take your time. I'll just grab a quick nap while you're busy spending money."

"Even better."

With my seat laid back in her luxury sedan, the rhythmic rocking of the car lulls me to sleep almost as soon as I close my eyes. The seat warmer acts like an electric blanket underneath me in the still cool April air—at least, it feels chilly to me. With chemo, I seem to be cold all the time, while other women in what we call our "chemo clique" burn up with hot flashes. Every *body* is definitely different in how it responds and reacts to medications and the nearly lethal cocktails.

The shopping trip must have zapped my energy more than I realized. I didn't feel the car stop. I didn't hear the opening and closing of the door when Mom left the car. I didn't even know when she returned and drove off with me. I wake from the best nap I've had in ages when she gently shakes my shoulder.

"Grace, wake up, sweetheart. We're here."

"Here?" I ask, my voice thick with sleep. "Where's here?"

As the electric seatback rises, my eyes try to focus, and my brain tries to understand the scene in front of me. Mom unlocks the doors, and Blake is suddenly kneeling beside me.

"Hi, beautiful. Did you have a good time with your mom?"

"Yeah, it was fun. What's going on, Blake? Why are we at an airport?"

"This is part of your surprise, babe. Your parents chartered a private jet, and we're all going away for a few days."

"Who's all going away?"

"You, Kyle, your parents, my parents, and me. We're having an entire family vacation. Leigh and Alex are also joining us as part of our extended family."

"That's right, sunshine. Now get your lazy ass out of that car, and let's hop on the private jet. I've never been on one, and I can't wait to take a million selfies onboard." Leigh strolls up beside Blake, and Alex steps up behind her. "Your husband has gone to a lot of trouble to spoil you. I mean, surprise you. Let's go."

"I don't have any clothes or anything, Blake."

"Yes, you do, Mom. You have an entire trunk full of them— even bathing suits," Kyle steps up behind Blake, his smile beaming with his pride. "We're all in on this surprise, and we've got you covered. You don't have to do anything but have a good time."

"It seems I'm outnumbered *and* being kidnapped. Maybe I should just go along with my captors and try to enjoy myself for a few days, huh?"

"That would be best. I can always throw you over my shoulder and carry you to the plane if that makes you feel like you resisted." The playful gleam in Blake's eyes and the cocky grin on his face leave no doubt he'd gladly accomplish his threat.

"I'll walk, but I'll need you to twist my arm a little harder."

He leans in the car and presses his lips to mine. His tongue sweeps across the part in my lips, and my traitorous body immediately responds to his touch. My mouth opens, inviting him in. His kiss is slow, methodical, and delicious. He knows he has me right where he wants me—eating out of the palm of his hand, melting into the plush leather seat, and following him wherever he wants to take me.

"How was that for coercion?"

"Perfect. I couldn't resist that even if I tried."

I swing my legs out of the car, and he takes my hand, helping me up as he stands and closes the door behind me. My chest skims along his as I straighten my legs, and he wraps one arm around my waist, holding me against him. "Are you okay, babe? Your mom said you were out of it all the way over here."

"I'm okay. I guess I just didn't realize I was so tired. But that nap hit the spot, and I feel good now."

He studies me for a few seconds, trying to decide if I'm hiding symptoms from him. "Promise you'll tell me when you start feeling tired, and you'll rest in between activities?"

"I promise, honey. I'll even make you come to bed with me."

"Then we won't get much rest, I'm afraid." He waggles his eyebrows at me and flashes that stunning smile of his that makes butterflies flutter in my stomach.

We turn and follow the others toward the chartered jet waiting at the private airstrip. His arm stays wrapped around me, holding me tight against him, as if his greatest fear is letting me go. But who am I to talk when my arms are wrapped around his waist and I'm stuck to his body much like our matching tattoo?

I understand his fear firsthand. Every day, every new symptom, every new pain steals a breath away from me. But my husband's love and care give it back to me. How I ever thought I'd get through this without depending on him is beyond me.

We climb the steps to the private plane, and from the moment I see the interior, I'm stunned speechless. I've never seen such opulence and luxury. Every piece of new technology I could ever want or need—and some I have no idea what to do with—are inside. Lush leather reclining chairs and couches are scattered throughout. A flight attendant greets us and offers a preflight drink.

I feel Blake's eyes on me as I turn in a full circle and take in every single detail I can. When I look up at him, emotions I've kept in check threaten to overcome me. "I can't believe you've planned all this for me. I don't expect this treatment, but I want you to know how much I appreciate it...how much I appreciate you. If we'd stayed home and made s'mores in the backyard, I would be happy because I'd be with you."

"I know, babe. You've never been high-maintenance. But for the next week, you'll finally know what it feels like to be the queen—my queen."

CHAPTER 21

Grace

No one will tell me where this plane will land. They won't even let me look out the window in case I figure it out before we get there. Even the flight attendant has been sworn to secrecy and only smiles sweetly when I try to press her for information. I've given up on trying to get someone to let it slip and decided to enjoy the ride, wherever they may take me. When the pilot announces we're beginning our descent for landing, I'm so excited I can barely contain myself.

We step out onto the tarmac of the small, private airport, and the heat instantly engulfs me. Small beads of sweat pop up on my skin from the high humidity. We have to be near a beach—there's no way we're anywhere that doesn't have lots of sun, sand, and surf. This day just keeps getting better and better.

I grab Blake's hand and drag him behind me to one of the waiting limousines. "Kyle, come on, son. We don't have all day."

"Nope. We have all week, Mom."

We pile into the line of luxury cars, and I watch anxiously out the window for signs telling me where we've landed. Blake chuckles from beside me, knowing exactly what I'm doing.

"I wanted to take you somewhere exotic and tropical, but not everyone had enough forewarning to get passports in time for the trip. Plus, I'm not so sure that's a good idea with your chemo anyway. So, we're in Florida, headed for Madeira Beach to have some fun, throw in a few surprises, and still have some time alone." Blake pulls the back of my hand to his lips. "Maybe we'll just have dinner and relax on the beach tonight, though. You've had a long day. You need to be rested up for tomorrow."

"What's tomorrow?"

He just smiles at me, not falling for my obvious trick. I snuggle into him and watch the scenery as we drive out of the touristy part of town and into a less populated area. When we pull into the lavish beachfront villa, I feel like we've been transported to a tropical island. Palm trees line the private drive. A huge pool area overlooks the white sand beach and clear turquoise water. Blake tries to hide his pleased smile when he sees the wonder in my eyes, but I know pride swells in his chest.

"There's still a little while of daylight left. Why don't you step out and take a look around for a minute? I'll be right back, babe."

I slide out of the back seat with him and walk across the boardwalk that leads over the sand dunes and to the open beach. The waves break and the white crest of water rolls in, one after the other, gently lapping the shore. The peaceful roar belies the power the water contains just underneath the surface, but it has a calming effect on me. With my eyes closed, I can discern each distinct sound around me...and I almost feel at home.

"My God. You take my breath away, Grace. You have the most beautiful, serene expression on your face. Your whole body looks relaxed and free of all the stress you've been under lately."

He's so close, I feel his breath on my cheek when he speaks. I inhale his masculine cologne and feel his inherent strength as if it were my own. His arms wrap around me, tentatively at first until I pull him closer. Now, *this* feels like home.

"I haven't even seen the room, but it doesn't matter. This place feels magical."

"I should've brought you here years ago." A touch of forlorn regret tints his voice.

"No regrets over what has passed, Blake. We live in the now and plan for the future. And right now, I'm in heaven here with you, and I haven't even stepped foot in the ocean yet."

"Let's fix that right now, then."

We walk forward together and stand in ankle-deep water, letting the waves pull the sand from beneath our feet with every surge. When our legs are buried up to our ankles, I turn my head to look up at him. "Looks like you're stuck with me, Blake Hardy."

"Perfect. There's nowhere else I'd rather be, and no one else I'd rather be stuck with, Grace Hardy."

I lean back against his chest as he holds me up, safe and secure in his arms, and watch the sun set behind the horizon. If only this moment could last forever.

"Blake, we're going up to the condo to sort out all the luggage, make sure it gets to the right places. I'm sure the bellhop put all the bags in one room. You have the key cards, right? Gretchen and Anna are itching to unpack everything and get it all sorted out. You two stay out here in the ocean breeze and take it easy," Dad says.

"Sure, Matt. Thank you. I'll take you up on that offer and keep Grace buried in the sand with me. There's a card in here for everyone."

When I open my eyes and look over at my dad, I realize everyone is out here with us. I mean *everyone*—my parents, Blake's parents, Kyle, Leigh, and Alex. I don't know how long I've been standing here, ignoring the world while I disappear into the ocean's depths. But now I realize I've also held them hostage out here with me.

"I'm sorry, guys—I'm so rude! I've been standing here like the world is my oyster and didn't even consider anyone else. We can help with unpacking the luggage and putting up the clothes."

"Nonsense. We love it out here as much as you do. If we didn't want to be out here, we already would've said something. And no, you cannot help us with the luggage or anything else. You stay out here and soak it all in as long as you want," Dad replies. "Don't argue with your father, little girl."

"He's right, Grace. There are plenty of us here to take care of the bags," Jeffery replies with a wink.

When Dad hands out the room keys, he gives one set back to Blake. "These are for your condo."

"We have a separate one?" I ask.

"Yeah, we sure do, babe. Our parents and Kyle are staying in one three-bedroom condo. Alex and Leigh have their own, and we have our own. But they're all on the same floor, so we're still close. Don't worry about a thing—we've thought of everything. Trust me."

I'm a little too pleased that Blake and I have a separate room from the rest of our entourage. Not that I don't want to spend time with our extended family, but while we're at the beach, I need some time alone with my man too.

"Let's have a seat in the sand," Blake murmurs against my cheek.

"Okay. Lead the way."

He picks out a seat with a view and pulls me down in front of him, resting between his legs. He moves the tails of my scarf out of the way to press sensual kisses on the back of my neck.

"I know you," he says then kisses me again.

"You'll have a million questions tomorrow."

More kisses.

"But we won't give you any answers."

The warmth of his tongue on my skin sends waves of electricity throughout my body.

"You should just go ahead and accept that this is the way it has to be."

Oh my God, that was a full lick up my spine. Goose bumps cover my arms, and my heart flutters.

"And let me spoil you, take care of you, and surprise you at every turn."

Holy hell, his teeth grazing the sensitive skin of my neck drives me crazy. My toes curl and my fingers grip his legs as he moves up and down the side of my neck with wet kisses and teasing bites while he waits for me to surrender to him.

"Mmm." I can't control the moans he elicits from deep inside me. He knows exactly what to do to me. He always has.

"Does that mean you agree?" Without giving me time to answer, he dives back in, biting me then sucking my skin into his mouth.

"Yes," I manage to reply in a pant.

I feel him smile against my skin. "That's what I wanted to hear. But now there are a lot more sounds I need to hear you make."

He slides his hand down between my legs, and my knees widen of their own accord, giving him all the space he wants. I turn my face to his, and he immediately takes my mouth, his tongue sliding across mine with frantic need. He slips his hand inside my pants then under my panties. When he thrusts a finger inside me, my hips buck upward, giving him access to push even deeper. At the curl of his finger, I come undone under his touch and involuntarily cry out in ecstasy.

"That was so fucking hot, Grace. I can't wait until later tonight when I have you all to myself in our room. But right now, we have to go get ready for dinner with the family. Do you feel up for it?"

"If I have to. I'd rather spend the time with you stealing all my energy instead."

"Stop tempting me." With more restraint than I possess, Blake stands and pulls me to my feet. "Let's go eat, then I'll have dessert when we get back to our room. Speaking of, you haven't even seen it yet. Come with me, my love."

~

Blake

WE WALK BACK into the room after dinner, and Grace kicks her heels off as soon as she's across the threshold.

"Unzip me." She turns around and offers me her back.

I slide down the zipper of her little black dress, letting my fingers graze her bare skin as the fabric separates. Without thinking, I lean in and follow the trail with my lips and tongue. Her dress falls to the floor into a pool at her feet before I scoop her up in my arms and carry her to the bedroom.

We left the bedroom balcony door open to enjoy the ocean scents and sounds before we went to dinner. The balmy temperature in the bedroom helps keep Grace warm, but the small beads of sweat that pop up on her skin become my aphrodisiac. After I deposit her in the center of the bed, I shed my clothes as fast as I can. In an instant, my mouth is on her, flattening my tongue against her soft slit and licking up to her clit. Circling around it, I increase the pressure, and her fingers grip my head.

"Blake, I need you inside me now. I don't want to wait."

Positioned at her wet entrance, my cock throbs from the heat emanating from her pussy. I slide into her slowly at first, relishing the wet softness, the way her body stretches to take all of me, and how her fingernails dig into my skin from the intense pleasure. Once I'm fully seated to her hilt, I lean down to her ear and whisper, "Hold on to me, babe. I'll make sure you sleep well tonight after I drain every ounce of energy from your body."

With the intensity of a madman, I repeatedly drive into her, turning and flipping her in every imaginable position as I claim every climax her body has to offer. The warm room only adds fuel to my fire. The sweat of our bodies mixes, our slick bodies slide against each other in an erotic dance. Her name falls from my lips when her inner walls grip me tighter. With my every pump into her, she responds with louder cries until she can no longer hold out, and the buildup inside her releases like a dam breaking. My release follows closely behind hers, and we fall onto the bed in a heap of tangled limbs.

Before I reach over to turn off the lamp, she's already sound asleep beside me. She curls into me, her arm crosses my body, and her grip tightens around me without conscious effort. With only the light of the moon streaming in through the wall of glass, I watch her sleep. My fingers brush over her cooling skin as I lie awake thinking about our life together. The life we've created since the day I almost gave her up for good. I've changed so much since then—or maybe I just realized what I had, what I almost lost, and reverted to the man I already knew I was. The man she deserved to have all along—the one who loves her unconditionally.

But everything I do now is to make all of that up to her. This week will be a major step in that direction. I can't wait until she experiences all the events we have planned. If she has any lingering doubts about my feelings for her, she won't after I'm done. Then every day for the rest of my life, she'll feel the depth of my love for her. I'll make damn sure of that.

CHAPTER 22

Grace

The bright Florida sun fills the room and wakes me from a deep sleep. I roll over and snuggle into a warm, hard body. When I finally manage to pry my eyes open, I'm surprised to find it's already almost ten in the morning. We haven't slept this late in years. Though, after last night's romp between the sheets, I needed the rest.

"Good morning, beautiful."

"Good morning, my lover," I say while I stretch and yawn. "Did you sleep well?"

"Yeah, when I finally fell asleep, I slept like a rock. Seems you did too. You were out before I could reach the lamp."

"It's your fault. You wore me out." I lay my head on his shoulder and hear the rumble of his chuckle through his chest.

"Sorry, but I'm not sorry about that. I plan to help you sleep that well every night."

"I'm going to hold you to your word."

"I'll give you something to hold, all right."

I've missed our fun and sexy banter. It feels so good to have it back.

"Don't worry, honey. I'll hold it all you want tonight."

"I need you to put that in writing," he chuckles. "But for now, it's time to get ready. Your mom has big plans for you this morning. I sent her a text and let her know you were sleeping in. But if you keep her waiting much longer, she'll start banging on the door."

"You're not coming with us?"

"Not this morning. I have a few things to take care of around here. You'll be back here with me before you know it. Go have fun with Gretchen, my mom, and Leigh. They love you too."

"I'll go this morning, but I refuse to leave you every day when we are finally on vacation at the beach. The rest of the week is ours together."

"If you insist," he teases with an exaggerated roll of his eyes. "I guess I can squeeze you into my busy schedule."

"Smartass." I laugh as I get up and head toward the shower.

"You love my smart ass, and you know it."

I stop and wait for his gaze to meet mine. "I do love you, Blake. I don't say this enough, but you've always been in my heart. No matter what the future holds, I want you to remember that."

"You own all of me, Grace, all my love. Until the end of time."

Mom, Anna, and Leigh are waiting when Blake and I emerge from our room.

"Could you two be more like newlyweds? Hanging all over each other, kissing, being all lovey-dovey all the time. Public displays of affection are frowned upon by most people, you know." Leigh shifts her weight to one leg, juts her hip out, and puts her hand on her waist.

"Then it's a good thing we don't care what most people think, isn't it?" Blake replies with a shameless smile for Leigh.

"Can I have my best friend now? Or do we need to have you two surgically separated?"

"You can *borrow* her—but only for a little while. I'll need her back soon, or I'll have to come find her."

Leigh rolls her eyes and loops her arm with mine, pulling me out from under Blake's hold. "We're having a girls' day today. No boys allowed. Sorry."

Blake places a lingering kiss against my temple. "Have fun today without me. Don't overdo it, though. If you need to rest, make them sit down with you for a while."

"I will—don't worry about me. What are you doing today?"

"Kyle, Alex, Dad, Matt, and I have plans for a male-bonding day while you girls are out having fun. I'll see you this evening. Love you, babe."

"Love you too."

"That's enough of that. I'm going to be sick from all this sugary-sweet shit." Leigh begins walking away, pulling me with her, while the chorus of laughter echoes off the walls.

We slide into the back of the waiting limo, and I look expectantly at my girlfriends for the day. "Where are we going? What are we doing? What's going on? Someone has to tell me!"

"First, we're going to get your hair done. You haven't done anything with it in forever," Leigh says with a straight face.

We lock eyes for a second before I burst out laughing. "Leave it to you to break the ice."

"I'm glad I'm good for something. Your mom has a wonderful day planned for us, so we're just going to follow her lead."

"Mom, spill it."

"Leigh isn't far off base. We're having a fun twist on a spa day. You've been under a lot of stress lately, and you deserve to be pampered for a while. There's an upscale spa nearby that offers so many services—hair, nails, makeup, massages, saunas, hot tubs. If it helps you relax, they have it. Only so many people are allowed in per day, so you can have as many of the services as you want."

"That sounds perfect. I can't wait. Right now, all those choices are calling my name. The only thing I don't know is which service to have first."

"We *may* have already made all the appointments for the day," Anna chimes in. "We wanted to make sure we were able to make the rounds to all the areas before they close. This is for you, sweetheart, and we want you to enjoy every second of it."

"I'm sure I will, Anna. I've never been to a spa before, so I'm just thrilled to finally get the full treatment. I'm glad all of you are going with me, too. This is our first all-girls' day together."

The facility is behind a gated drive to keep anyone without an appointment from disrupting the serenity for those inside. The sprawling estate is immaculate, with thick green grass, clusters of palm trees providing shade for the swinging hammocks, and small, zero entry pools dotting the landscape for a private oasis. We haven't even stepped foot inside the building inspired by ancient Roman architecture yet, but I already know we won't ever want to leave.

A personal concierge greets us at the door and introduces herself as Julie. Our limo driver steps up behind us and hands the bellhop several small suitcases and garment bags. No one meets my questioning gaze when I move my eyes from my mom to Leigh then to Anna. Julie takes us on a tour of the facility, showing us where all the amenities are located, before escorting us to a large changing room.

"This changing room is only for your party. Your bags are already here. You can store your valuables in the lockers—just take the wristband key with you. You're also free to use the robes and slippers. Let any of our staff members know if we can do anything to make your day more relaxing."

"All right, ladies. Let's change into our robes and get our full-body massages to start the day off right," Anna says.

The Asian-themed massage room is cool and inviting, with four massage tables lined along the long wall in front of covered windows. Cloth blinds filter the harsh light from outside to maintain the tranquility inside. The beds are separated by chest-high partitions for privacy, but the open space above allows for conversations. The therapists explain what we can expect before telling us to lie facedown on the tables. When they leave the room to give us privacy to disrobe, I turn to Mom.

"Did you arrange for us to do all of our activities together today?"

"Yes. I hope you don't mind. I just want us to spend as much time together as we can. This is a special trip, and I want to remember every minute of it."

"No, I don't mind at all. I'm actually relieved, to be honest. I was afraid I'd go into the wrong room and embarrass myself."

The sheets on the massage table are the softest I've ever felt. After I sink down into the covers, I breathe out slowly, fully exhaling and letting the stress leave my body. The scents and sounds in the room add to the overall ambiance. Knowing my family is so close provides another level of comfort.

All the years we've wasted with petty disagreements and insignificant differences still trouble me occasionally, but I push those feelings aside and focus on my life at this moment. When they said they were going to spoil me this week, they weren't kidding. I could easily get used to this life—a marriage forged in the fires and bonded by steel. A close-knit family that includes in-laws and best friends. My teenage son, willingly spending his senior year spring break with his mom, dad, and grandparents instead of going away with his friends.

This is the life I've always wanted.

Two hours later, after the sea salt exfoliation scrub and the full-body massage is over, I'm too relaxed to move. If I could just stay in this room the rest of the day, I could go back to the hotel a very happy woman. But the demanding women I came here with reject my plan and force me to leave my comfortable place. With my robe belt tied securely around my waist and my complimentary slippers on my feet, I follow them to the next room, wondering what awaits me.

"Welcome, welcome. You ladies must be the Baldwin-Hardy-Brydon party." An immaculately dressed woman steps out from behind the counter and warmly greets each of us. Her hair is perfectly coiffed, and her makeup looks professionally applied. Her long, slender fingers are tipped in a beautiful French manicure. Her smile is genuine, and her presence is inviting. She loves her job, and it shows in her manner.

"We are. You must be Monica," Mom says and extends her hand.

"And you must be Gretchen. It's nice to meet you in person finally."

"Monica, I can't tell you how much I appreciate you coming in for us on your off day. Wilma has been a dear friend of mine for years, and she insisted no one else would do except you."

"That's very kind of her to say. It really was no problem at all. I simply switched days with another of our artists, and I have to tell you, it worked out much better for me in the long run." Her laugh is genuine, and I immediately feel at ease with Monica. Some people just click as soon as they meet. She seems to be one of those people who can click with anyone.

"This is my daughter, Grace. Next to her is Anna, Grace's mother-in-law. And that young lady beside Anna is Leigh, Grace's best friend since they were little kids."

Monica moves to each of us as Mom makes introductions, shaking our hands and reciting her polite hellos. When she first looked at me, I didn't see any shock over my baldness in her expression. That makes me wonder how much Mom told her before we arrived.

"I'm so glad to meet all of you. I'm honored you chose me to handle such a momentous day. All four of you here together for the first time, getting pampered and probably putting yourselves first for the first time in forever. Come inside my studio, and let's get started. I'm excited about what we're doing today!"

Again, no one will even glance at me to explain the cryptic meaning behind Monica's words. Instead, I'm ushered first through the door and into what she referred to as her studio. The room is brighter than the reception area. One side of the room has thick, padded electric lounge chairs, while the other has full-service hair salon chairs. Pedicure chairs and nail technician stations sit at the far end of the room. This is a luxury full-service room at its finest.

"Grace, make yourself comfortable in one of the lounge chairs, and I'll be right with you. Gretchen and Anna, you're both starting at the salon stations. Leigh, we're going to start you with a manicure and pedicure. As we finish with each of you, you'll just move to the next station—except for you, Grace. You're with me the whole time."

I'm not sure what Monica plans to do to me, but I do as she says and make myself comfortable on the padded lounge chair. She pulls a wheeled chair up beside me and makes small talk while she lays out a variety of products on a mobile table. When she has it all arranged, she turns to me.

"When your mom called and asked me to be here today, she told me all about your condition. I want to be upfront with you about that and say I completely understand what you're going through. My mom also had breast cancer and lost all her hair from the chemotherapy. I was very grateful I could use my skills to help her. Are you ready to get started?"

"What are we doing, exactly? I don't know what your skills are. Everyone is keeping secrets from me today."

The sly smile that spreads across Monica's face says she knows the secret and also isn't telling. "I'm an aesthetician. I offer more than regular cosmetology services. For today, your mom asked me to give you a facial, airbrush your makeup, and apply synthetic eyelashes and eyebrows. Are you okay with all that?"

Am I okay with it? I want to cry I'm so happy. I've missed my eyelashes more than I ever realized I could. I took them for granted every day of my life for thirty-six years, until the day they all fell out, and I had to get used to living without them.

All I can do is nod my head. I don't want any tears today, especially since they'll ruin my makeup and new eyelashes.

Monica works on me the entire time. I hear the others chatting and changing places, but I'm happy in my chair with my personal aesthetician overseeing every detail of my face. From the facial that felt like a gentle massage and left my skin as soft as a baby's bottom, to the professionally applied airbrush makeup, to the fake eyebrows that will look real, to the eyelashes she's now gluing on my eyelids, I've been treated like royalty. I can't wait to open my eyes and see what she's called her masterpiece.

"Keep your eyes closed for a minute. The glue is drying, and the fumes can burn your eyes a little."

The lounge chair begins to move, raising my back up to sitting position. I'm so excited, I can hardly wait to open my eyes. From around the room, I hear a couple of gasps followed by someone making a shushing noise. Then sniffles. Dammit, now I know I'm going to cry and make a mess of my new face.

"Okay, Grace. I've moved the mirror directly in front of you. Open your eyes now."

The moment I've been waiting for is finally here.

My eyes slowly flutter open, and I immediately notice the weight of my new eyelashes. That gives me a giddy feeling. *I have eyelashes!*

Then I see the woman staring back at me. The woman in the mirror who has eyebrows, eyelashes, and perfect skin...but no hair. The fears I've pushed down deep inside me, that I've ignored and played off like they don't matter, come rushing to the surface all at once. I stare, expressionless with a calm exterior, but so many questions fly through my mind.

How will I ever be able to compete with Tammy in Blake's eyes?

She's younger, prettier, and healthier. I'll never be that woman again.

How can Blake ever be physically attracted to me again? I don't look the same anymore, and all the makeup and plastic in the world won't change that fact. Chances are, I'll be on chemotherapy for the rest of my life—what's left of it—and that means not only will I have no hair, but no eyelashes and no eyebrows either. No body hair of any kind.

How will I be confident enough to undress in front of him after I finish this regimen? When I have surgery—whether that's a lumpectomy or a mastectomy—there will be a period when my chest will be disfigured...uneven...ugly.

"Grace?" Mom almost whispers and slowly approaches me. "What do you think?"

What do I think?

I'm scared—to death.

"I think Monica is amazing," I reply, forcing a smile when I look up at her.

My gaze drops back to the woman in the mirror, and I force the tears back down my throat.

"You look gorgeous."

"Thanks, Mom."

"Ladies, can you give us a minute?" Leigh asks then sits down beside me. The others file out of the studio, back into the reception area. When we're alone, Leigh puts her hand on my shoulder. "Spill it. What's wrong?"

Since I can't bear to look in the mirror any longer, I turn to face her head on. Then I spew every fear, every thought, and every worry I've held inside.

"I've tried to be strong. I've tried to move past it and look on the bright side. I've tried to be grateful I'm still alive and my cancer is responding to treatment...so far. But everything just hit me all of a sudden, like a two-ton brick falling on my head. Before you give me the pep talk about it's what's inside that matters and all that other bullshit, I know all the platitudes. They're just words —they don't help."

Leigh nods and purses her lips while my rant sinks in. "Grace, I won't even pretend to know exactly how you feel. You know I'm vain as hell when it comes to my hair. I have an ugly shaped head. Without my hair, I'd scare all the little kids and most of the adults. Alex would have to go to every wig store and bring home every human-hair wig he could find. I'd hire the makeup artists from Hollywood to put the wig on me every day so it would stay and look natural. None of that showing net bullshit."

I can't help but start laughing, picturing Leigh doing everything she's threatened, and knowing without a doubt she would at least try.

"But here's the deal—and I'm being straight with you. I've never known a more beautiful woman than you. I've never *seen* a more beautiful woman. And neither has Blake. Hair or no hair. Eyebrows or no eyebrows. Eyelashes or no eyelashes. Makeup or no makeup. None of that matters. It's like the icing on top of the icing on top of the cake.

"Even with your momentary lapse in judgment and temporary nervous breakdown, you're still stronger than I ever will be. You're also smart enough to know all that bullshit you just told me is completely wrong. Now, if you're through with your pity party, we're on a tight schedule here, and you're keeping me from happy hour back at the hotel."

I grab her around the neck and hug her tightly. Because she's my best friend. She's the sister I never had. She's the one who can make me mad and make me laugh and make me forget my troubles all in one conversation. And I'm learning how important and vital my support system really is because there's no way I could face all of this without her with me.

"Grace, don't mess up my hair with your tears. You know what humidity does to it."

With a full belly laugh, I release her as I throw my head back.

"I'm not crying, you old bitch. That would mess up my eyelashes and my makeup."

"I'm here whenever you need me. You know that, Grace. But whether you have a full head of hair or none at all doesn't matter to Blake. Whether you have a triple-D rack or have to wear a training bra, he doesn't care. He loves you regardless of all that.

"You'll get brand-new boobs, and you'll want to touch them more than he does. You'll find a treatment that doesn't make all your hair fall out, and you'll be cursed with naturally curly hair when it grows back. Then you'll be happy. Or none of that will happen, but you'll still be happy. And Blake will still love you through it all. You're facing enough without worrying about vanity too. So, no more of that bullshit. Deal?"

"Deal."

CHAPTER 23

Blake

"Are you ready for this?" Matt asks.

I chuckle because he's more nervous than I am. In fact, I'm not nervous at all. But I am so excited I can't hardly stand it.

"I'm absolutely ready, Matt. Your daughter will be thrilled, and you'll do great. Don't sweat it." With a friendly clap on his shoulder, I walk around for the final check before the ladies return with my wife.

"Nothing's out of place, Dad. I just checked." Kyle walks up beside me and gives me a side-eye glance.

"I just want everything to be perfect for your mom. She deserves it."

"She does. She's been through so much, but she doesn't let it get her down. Not that I've ever seen anyway. I just want the worst to be behind us now."

"Never give up hope, son. Your mom won't, and I won't either. We may have setbacks now and then, but we'll keep pushing forward. And during the times when she feels like she can't take another step, I'll carry her. For as long as she needs me to."

He turns to face me. "Until the end of time?"

"Until the end of time."

"How did we get stuck doing all this? We should've taken Grace out deep-sea fishing or something and let the women oversee this part of the plan," Dad says as he walks up and slings his arm around my shoulders. "Did you volunteer us for this?"

"Wasn't me. It was Kyle's idea." I laugh at the expression on Kyle's face.

"Just throw me under the bus, Dad. Good job. Didn't you raise him better than this, Pops?"

"There's only so much parents can do, Kyle. The rest is up to the kid. We tried, though."

The three of us laugh together, and I realize how incredibly fortunate I am to have so many people who love me. Everyone who matters to me is here to celebrate one of the many things I've always wanted to be able to give Grace but haven't been able to until now. My family, friends who became family, and Grace's family. We don't have the huge extended family that some others do, but we're blessed with who we do have.

Matt rejoins us, his nervous energy visible on his face. "Blake, can I talk to you alone for a minute?"

"Sure, Matt."

We walk inside the empty banquet center we've reserved just for our small family. It's the perfect setting for Grace's surprise. Floor-to-ceiling windows line the wall facing the beach, giving the perfect view of the waves rolling in, the sun setting on the horizon, and backdrop for the family photoshoot wish Grace has on her Why Not list.

"Have a seat, Blake."

I sit, but Matt paces back and forth in front of me. His gaze is trained on the floor just in front of his feet, and he repeatedly runs his fingers over his mustache, around his mouth, then down to his chin.

"Matt, take a deep breath, slow down, and tell me what's on your mind. I feel like you're about to start running laps around the room any second now."

He turns on his heels and looks at me with a blank expression at first, then bursts out laughing at himself. "You're right, I need to calm down. To be honest with you, I just don't want to mess this up. We just got you, Grace, and Kyle back in our lives, and I don't want to offend you and lose you again."

"You're not going to offend me, Matt. Whatever it is, we'll talk through it like adults. We're all in this together now. All three of us want it to stay that way."

"I'm delighted to hear that. Gretchen and I have missed out on so much in your lives. That's what prompted me to come up with this idea in the first place. Gretchen and I had a long talk before we left to come down here, and she is fully on board with this proposal.

"After Grace explained her diagnosis and prognosis, we did some research of our own. Then I talked to a few of my doctor friends on the golf course and got as much information from them as they could give me without actually seeing her medical records. This whole situation has gutted me and made me reeval-uate almost everything in my life. I've given the board notice of my retirement at the end of the year. I'm leaving my position as CEO and President and will only be an active board member, so I'll have more time away from work.

"In all frankness, we don't know how much time Grace has before the tumors become unmanageable. I know something could happen to any of us at any time, but this is happening to my daughter right now, so that makes it much more real to me. I've tried to remain optimistic, but one nagging thought won't leave me alone, Blake. This is where my concern of offending you comes in."

"I'm listening, and I'm with you so far. What are you proposing?"

"Part of my executive package includes a hefty lump-sum compensation package when I retire, around $20 million. I want to give that money to you and Grace, so you both can quit your jobs and focus on her health and cross off every wish on your Why Not lists. Here's the thing, I know the average family in your situation isn't afforded this luxury. But I want to give this opportunity to *my* family because I'm able to, and it's the only item on my Why Not list. What I'm really asking of you is to take care of my little girl for the rest of her life, however long that may be."

"Matt, I'm floored, and I don't know what to say. This isn't at all what I expected when we walked in here to talk."

"Say yes. Give an old man some peace of mind in his twilight years. My intentions are somewhat selfish, I'll admit. The less time you two are at work, the more time we'll have to erase the pains of the past and make the present an even happier place."

How can I argue with that?

"All right, Matt. My answer is yes. Don't think I won't use all the guilt trips you just laid on me to convince Grace, though. She loves her job, so getting her to agree to quit won't be all that easy. You may have noticed she's also fiercely independent."

Matt smiles, and there's no hint of nervousness left in the man. "I have a feeling you'll be able to persuade her."

"I'll do my best. It's a little scary how you were able to push all the right buttons in me to get what you wanted, especially in such a short conversation."

"Son, I haven't been the CEO of a Fortune 100 company for the last thirty-five years without learning to read people and negotiate to get what I want." The smile that now covers his face is the one I imagine his business opponents see when they learn they've been bested by him. It's one of pure victory.

In this case, I'm more than willing to say I've been defeated.

"Dad, it's almost time. Let's go change clothes." Kyle leans into the room, his hand gripping the doorknob and the urgency in his voice making his tone rise an octave.

"Sounds like it's just about show time, Matt."

~

Grace

WITH THE MAKEUP CRISIS OVER, Mom leads our expedition on to the next adventure. We walk through the double French doors into a beautiful sunroom filled with enough green and flowering plants to make any gardener envious. The white, wrought-iron patio tables and chairs have the perfect balance of decoration to make the place settings stand out. The room simultaneously screams luxury and whispers relaxation. The all-glass walls provide an unobstructed view of the professionally manicured grounds and the tropical pools.

"This is beautiful," I gasp. "Think I can have a room like this built on to my house?"

"In Vermont? I don't think the view would quite match this one." Leigh laughs. "Maybe we should move somewhere warmer in the winter, join the snowbird movement."

"That wouldn't be so bad, would it?"

"Not so bad at all."

"Are you two ready for a quick bite to eat before we head back to the hotel? There's no telling what those men have been up to without chaperones for so long." Anna steps up beside me, admiring the view with us for a moment. "You're doing a good thing, Grace. Forgiving your mom and spending time with her now. You're a good daughter."

"It feels good to let go of everything and start over. You know I've always thought of you as my mom, too, right? Maybe I never told you outright, but I love you, and I'm lucky to have you in my life."

She raises her hand to cover her mouth, the emotions she can't voice swimming in her eyes. Then she grabs me in a full embrace, and the memories of the nights she held me while I cried over the broken relationship with my parents crop up in my mind. The pain I felt back then can't hurt me now, but my love for this wonderful woman increases every day. She took me in as a homeless, pregnant teenager and treated me like one of her own children. I'll never be able to repay her for that kindness.

"You've always been the daughter I never had, Grace. I've never seen you as anything different." When she releases me, she grabs a napkin and dabs her eyes. "Now stop trying to ruin my makeup. I know that's what you're trying to do."

"You're onto me. I want you all to have black mascara all over your faces. My new eyelashes would never betray me like that."

We're still giggling when we take our seats, order our meals, and enjoy the delicious food and company. Everyone but me has mimosas—chemotherapy drugs and alcohol don't play nice together. Those small concessions don't bother me, though. In the grand scheme of importance, it doesn't even rank. This trip has already been the best vacation of my life, and we're only on the second day. I'm mentally adding a few more entries on my Why Not list—activities that will be fun to do with Kyle while we're here.

"Grace?"

I look up to find three sets of eyes staring at me intently. "What? What'd I miss?"

"You were a million miles away just now. Where'd you go?" Mom asks.

"I was riding Jet Skis with Kyle in the Gulf of Mexico."

"Adding on to your Why Not list, huh?"

"Exactly. We should all go together tomorrow. It'll be fun."

"Can we finish what we have planned for today first?" Mom stands and holds out her hand. I take it and stand with her. "The last stop on our spa excursion is the best. And it's time. Come with me, sweetheart."

Anna and Leigh get up and follow us out of the sunroom café. Their uncontained giggles and loud whispers of excitement fuel my curiosity. What could be better than what we've already experienced today?

Two staff members stand in the hallway in front of the double doors leading into our private dressing room. Their broad smiles and eager observations match my family's excitement. They're so genuine I can't help but return the sentiments. Then they open both the doors at the same time—and I'm stunned speechless. My smile drops along with my bottom jaw, which is now touching the floor at my feet. Without even thinking about it, I cover my heart with my hand and feel it pounding inside my chest. Warm hands touch my back and gently push me forward since my feet and legs have forgotten how to walk.

"Blake came to see your daddy and me not long ago, and we had a long talk. He shared a lot with us—his past mistakes, his desire to atone for those mistakes, and his unconditional and unwavering love for you. This week is all about what he has always wanted to give you, but was never able to until now.

"He planned every step of it, Grace, and asked all of us to help him make it come true. When you shared your Why Not list with him, he said he knew fate put you two together and kept you together. This one item on your wish list spoke to his heart more than you know, but I think maybe now you have an idea of just how much."

"Oh my God," I gasp and attempt to move past the shock so my brain can absorb the sight in front of me.

Three walls of lockers are covered by one wedding dress after another. Some are as extravagant as what I'd picture true royalty wearing—dresses made for a princess with miles of silk, tulle, and jeweled bodices. Others are made with a simpler pattern and a more modern and chic impression, but no less beautiful. The other dresses fall in between the wide spectrum of possibilities of everything I could ever imagine.

"He wants you to pick out the wedding dress you like the best. He hasn't seen any of them, so whichever one you choose will be a surprise. You two will renew your vows tonight with the big wedding you always dreamed of having." Mom walks around the room, looking at each style, wiping one tear after another from her eyes. "We'll all be there with you this time."

"I have one thing to say about this," Leigh chimes in as she examines one of the dresses. "Alex better step up his game —and fast."

Leave it to my best friend to bring levity to this emotional experience. God, I love her.

"What time is my wedding?"

"Late this afternoon, but before sunset. Blake was concerned about sun sensitivity with your chemo medications," Anna says.

"Get naked, woman. You have a bazillion dresses to try on before we choose one."

"Before *we* choose?" I ask, lifting one fake eyebrow.

"Did I stutter? I don't think I did. Yes, *we*. That's what brides-maids are for." Leigh picks up one of the dresses and holds it out toward me. "Try this one on first."

Dress after dress is thrust at me to try on. The ones *we* decide against are quickly taken away by the spa staff members. Finally, we've whittled down the vast amount to the final two contestants —and the cuts and patterns are complete opposites. One is a princess gown with a sweetheart neckline and ruched back and crisscrossing pleats across the bust. The layered tulle skirt is full and has a court train extending off the back. The other is a halter-style top with a soft, lightweight fabric skirt that would flow easily in the breeze.

I stand back and stare at the two dresses, my eyes darting back and forth while I try to make a decision.

"You want my opinion?" Leigh asks.

"Yes."

"The beach dress is beautiful and elegant. You looked so vibrant in it, prancing around the room and watching the skirt move with ease. I loved it. But it was never your dream dress, Grace. Don't settle. Not for this special occasion. Not ever again."

Decision made.

∼

"WAIT HERE. DO NOT PEEK." Anna's eyebrows draw downward in a stern, motherly threat.

"No peeking. I promise."

After a couple of minutes, she returns with a huge clump of tissues in her hand. She gives half of them to my mother. "You'll need these. Come with me." Turning her gaze to me, she continues. "Grace, your escort will be here any second now. You're the most beautiful bride I've ever seen."

After Mom and Anna walk out, Dad walks in—and stops dead in his tracks. I've never seen my dad cry...until now.

"Grace, when you were little, I always dreaded the day I'd have to give you away to another man. I'll deliver you to your husband today, but now I know you'll always be my little girl."

"Oh, Daddy." That's all I can muster before the tears well up in my eyes and blur my vision.

He moves to stand in front of me while I whisk the tears away, and I realize he has a box in his hands.

"What's that?"

"This is something I had made specially for you. Since we can't pin your veil to your head, I thought you may want to wear this instead."

I pull the lid off the box and find myself stunned speechless once again by the thoughtfulness of my family. "Daddy, it's gorgeous."

The flower crown is made of huge, exotic flowers in varying

hues of pink, purple, and white, with underlying greenery and baby's breath to complete the look. The veil is sewn into the rim of the flower crown, securing it in place and covering the top of my head at the same time. It's perfect. And beautiful. And more than completes my dream of having the perfect wedding ensemble.

"You're gorgeous, precious. I wouldn't miss this for anything in the world. Are you ready to go see Blake?"

"I'm ready."

Daddy leads me through the winding walkway toward the beach, and that's when I see what they've been up to while we were at the spa. A pergola has been transformed into a wedding chapel. The wood structure is completely covered in flowers that match the flower crown on my head. Ropes of flowers are attached to the guest chairs lining the aisle. Faces I don't recognize fill the seats, and I realize my family must have invited the other guests and beachgoers to join our festivities.

All eyes are on me.

They're all smiling at me.

I'm trying to take it all in and focus at the same time, but it's difficult because so many emotions fly through me at once. Then my gaze lands on Blake. Beside him, as his best man, is our son. Then my erratic thoughts calm, and I can focus on what's most important.

My whole world waits for me at the end of the aisle.

When we reach Blake and Kyle, Daddy turns to me and kisses my cheek. "I love you, precious. No matter how old you are, you'll always be my baby girl. But this time, I'm doing what I should have done in the first place and trusting Blake to love you, care for you, and cherish you every day for the rest of his life. I have faith in him, Grace. He won't let you or me down."

Daddy steps back and takes his seat, then Blake lifts my hands to his lips. He places soft, reverent kisses along my knuckles. "I love you," he whispers.

Before I can reply, he turns to the crowd that's gathered to watch us.

"Grace and I have been married for eighteen years. Ideally, I would've preferred to renew our vows on our wedding anniversary, but today is another anniversary of a very special day."

He turns to look at me, his dazzling smile melting my heart all over again, and he continues. "Today is the anniversary of our first date twenty years ago. Grace was a junior, and I was a senior in high school. The first time I saw her, I was a goner. She stole my heart and my breath. When she agreed to marry me, I thought I was the luckiest guy alive. Now that I'm older and I realize marriage licenses don't have an expiration date, I *know* I'm the luckiest man alive. Otherwise, she may have just let it lapse and gotten rid of me."

The crowd chuckles along with us as I shake my head from side to side, but I notice a few of the girls wiping their eyes through their smiles.

"Grace and I are renewing our vows and our commitments to each other because we've recently learned the hard way what a precious gift time is. That's why we don't have a preacher or anyone to officiate—I've written my own vows for my wife."

A moment of panic hits me because I haven't written any vows. I didn't know I was supposed to write them. Then I take a deep breath and remember this is *my* Blake standing beside me. My vows come from my heart, not my head.

"Grace, I promise to love, honor, and cherish you until the day I die. There will never be another woman for me as long as I live. Every day, I will remind you of my love for you and only you. The only tears I'll cause you to shed will be tears of happiness. For the rest of my days, I'll never hurt you or leave you. I promise to take care of you when you're sick, to reassure you when you're insecure, and to comfort you when you're scared.

"If I ever wake up alone and have to face the rest my days without you by my side, I'll carry your memory in my heart and in my mind. Your love, generosity, and kindness are unmatched by anyone else in this world. You'll always be the first and last person I think of every day, and the only woman who will ever own my heart."

He drops down to one knee, removes the single gold band that has served as my wedding band for the last eighteen years, and hands it to Kyle. Then he takes a black velvet box from Kyle's hand and lifts his eyes to meet mine.

"I've had these for a while now. They were originally meant to be a Christmas present, but you weren't ready to accept them at that time. I hope you are ready for them now."

He opens the box to show me the most beautiful set of wedding rings I've ever laid eyes on. He holds the diamond circled wedding band up first.

"This circle represents my unending love for you. There's no beginning and no end—it's eternal."

Then he presents the engagement ring.

"This ring represents our past, present, and future. The past is behind us, but it serves as a reminder of how far we've come together. Our present is our now—where we live, love, and play. Where we talk, share, and laugh. Where we grow closer, grow old together, and face every obstacle as one. Our future only holds happiness, regardless of what may come, only made possible because of our past and present."

He slides the rings onto my finger, and they fit perfectly. As if they were made just for me.

"I didn't give my wife any advance notice of what I had planned, so you'll have to forgive her for not having any vows to recite back to me. She only needs to answer my questions with one correct answer, though."

"Grace, do you promise to love, honor, and cherish me for the rest of your life? Do you promise to help me every day to be a better man, to be more like you? Do you promise to walk beside me, no matter how hard the road is, regardless of how trying the days are, and allow me to carry you when your burdens are too heavy? Do you promise to take all of my love with you wherever you go?"

"I do."

Blake stands and crushes his mouth to mine, pouring his love into me with every swipe of his tongue against mine. Telling me how much he loves me with each second that passes. Showing the world how much I mean to him with the lengths he's gone to to make this day extra special for me.

"You've made me the happiest woman alive, Blake. I love you so much."

He shakes his head lightly. "You healed my broken soul, Grace. You saved me from myself. You showed me what real love is, what real strength is, and what real family is. I would be nothing without you, and I'll never let you go. You're my saving grace."

EPILOGUE

"Just over four years ago, during what should've been the most carefree time of my life, I was forced to face immortality. During a time when every teenager believes he's invincible and nothing bad can touch him, I came face-to-face with the grim truth that there's no such thing as invincibility. While my friends were hanging out together, shooting basketball, playing video games, or spending all their spare time with their girlfriends—anything to avoid being stuck at home with their parents—I actively searched for ways I could spend more time with mine.

"When I started applying for colleges in my senior year of high school, my mom urged me to pursue the best. She taught me to set my sights high and to do everything within my power to accomplish everything I wanted out of life. If that meant I had to leave the state and go to college across the country, she would've supported that decision. If I started to question my decisions, she almost always had the same reply. She said, 'Kyle, you have to be happy with your life. I can't do that for you. What would make you happy?' Those words guided me through more decisions than I can count or remember.

"My friends applied to schools all over the country, coast to coast. Without telling my mom, I applied for colleges near home because I couldn't bear the thought of leaving her. After all the years she'd taught me to stand on my own two feet and not worry about her when I left for college, I just couldn't do it when the time came. I couldn't leave her.

"Some of you are thinking I'm a mama's boy, and you'd be right. But not for the reasons you may believe. You see, four years ago, my mom was diagnosed with breast cancer. That alone is scary enough. But then she received even worse news. What's worse than a breast cancer diagnosis, you ask? A metastatic breast cancer diagnosis. By the time they found the first tumor, the malignancy had already spread to her lung.

"For those of you who are unaware, metastatic breast cancer is currently a death sentence. Every woman is different. Every cancer is different. The timetable depends on the status of the metastasis. But, as my mom explained to me, the disease eventually kills everyone who has it. That's a sobering fact for a seventeen-year-old young man who relied on his mother for most everything, regardless of how big and tough he thought he was.

"For my spring break that year, our extended family brought Mom to the Tampa area for a surprise vacation. She'd already been through so much by that time, and we wanted her to have some fun and relax. It turned out to be the best vacation we'd ever had. My parents renewed their vows on the beach. Mom and I rode Jet Skis, body-surfed the waves, and took a deep-sea fishing trip. That week changed our lives in many ways. My parents decided to move to the area after I graduated high school, making my decision to leave Vermont an easy one.

"I've been asked the same question many times over the course of my last four years here at this college. 'Kyle, what gives you such a drive to succeed?' My reply was always something noncommittal and vague because the real answer felt too personal to discuss at the time. I can now sum it up in two words, though: my mom."

"You see, when I was worried about keeping my grades up and passing my tests, my mom was undergoing surgery that would change her body for the rest of her life. When my class load was considerably more than the average student and I thought I'd never have time to myself again, my mom was treating her burns after undergoing several weeks of radiation therapy. When I was tempted to complain about my unfair professors to anyone who would listen, I thought about the disappointment my mom felt when the oncologist said he had to change her chemotherapy regimen because it was no longer working.

"And every single time my mom faced those problems, she did so without complaint. She's human, so I'm sure she had moments when she wanted to give in and have a gigantic pity party. If she did, no one else ever knew it. If my mom could do that while fighting for her life, then I could refrain from feeling sorry for myself as a healthy young man in a comfortable college class.

"I kept that same attitude through every difficult class, every disappointing grade, every failure I experienced. Regardless of what I faced, I thought about how my mom would handle it. What would she tell me to do? Then I'd square my shoulders and face it head on. Now you know what drives me to excel, where my empathy for others originates, and most importantly, why I'm proud to be a mama's boy. I'll wear that title as long as I live.

"Because of my mom, I attended my first-choice college. Because of my mom, I'm graduating summa cum laude. Because of my mom, I've already been accepted into medical school. Because of my mom, I plan to dedicate my life to helping other families in similar circumstances. Because of my mom, I started a Why Not list at seventeen, and I've checked at least one thing off my list every single day. Because of my mom, many of you have also started a Why Not list, and have also made it an important part of your daily routine.

"My prayer is that she'll continue to defy the odds and be there to watch me become a doctor. Then I'll keep going until I find a way to cure her, because I'm selfish and I can't imagine my world without her in it.

"As we go forward in our endeavors, whether that means graduate school or straight into a job, there's one piece of advice I'd be honored if you'd take with you. None of your accomplishments will fulfill you the way the love of your family does. Don't ever take them for granted."

～

Grace

WHEN KYLE FINISHES his speech at honors night, I'm a blubbering mess. He didn't warn me beforehand, so I was not prepared for his words in the slightest. He poses for pictures with the other students graduating with honors, then makes his way over to Blake and me.

"What'd you think of my speech, Mom?"

My reply is to wrap my arms around my son's neck and hug him tightly. He slips his arms around my waist and easily lifts my feet off the floor. I miss the days when he was little. I'd give anything to go back in time and start all over again. While there are so many things I'd do differently in my life given the chance, having Kyle isn't one of them.

"You never told me you were going to give up going to school here and stay in Vermont."

"Because I knew you'd try to talk me out of it. I never would've left you, Mom."

"We're so proud of you, son. You're the best of both of us," Blake says with pride.

"You've both taught me so much about perseverance, even

when you didn't think there was any way you'd succeed. I saw that when you two stayed together instead of divorcing."

Blake and I exchange glances then turn our gazes back to Kyle. "I didn't realize you knew anything about that."

"I know you didn't. I never let on—not really. But I watched, I listened, and I learned from both of you."

"That's not a time I'm proud of, Kyle. I wish we'd had a chance to talk about it so you didn't think too badly of me, though," Blake says.

"No need to worry, Dad. I figured out what Mom was doing, and I knew it was important to her. Then the more time we spent together, the more I realized it was important to me too. Besides, it's good for kids to see their parents aren't perfect, but they still do their best despite their shortcomings. I love you both, and I'm proud to be your son."

Blake and I go back to our hotel room and leave Kyle to celebrate with his friends. Over the last four years of empty-nesting, Blake and I have grown closer than we ever imagined. Kyle was my main focus for the first eighteen years, I don't deny that. But now, Blake has my full attention, and I have his. The happiness we've brought each other outshines the bad, and we're stronger for it.

We live life one day at a time, one moment at a time, and check one item off our Why Not list every day. It serves as both a reminder that we're not the people we used to be, we're not yet the people we will be, but we both live for the now. Because now is all we have.

Take a hot air balloon ride. Check.

Build a sand castle. Check.

Go on a tour of Italy. Check.

Give others a reason to remember my name. Check.

Live long enough to see my son graduate from college. Check.

Without a promise to the next day, why not do what makes us happy today? Until the end of our time.

FAITH, HOPE, & LOVE

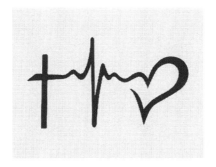

Until the end of time.

ACKNOWLEDGMENTS

This part is the hardest part of the book to write because I don't want to leave anyone out or make anyone feel unappreciated. I am so grateful for everyone who supports me in this endeavor. Singling people out for their specific support is my way of saying an extra special THANK YOU for their unwavering help.

First and foremost, I want to thank my Lord and Savior for His continued forgiveness of a sinner.

To my husband – I love you. Thank you standing beside me and helping me every step of the way.

Readers – I am so grateful for each and every single one of you! Without your constant support and willingness to shout from the rooftops about your favorite books, none of these characters would have a chance to live, even for a moment, in this fictional world we love so much. From the bottom of my heart, thank you for everything! Candace, thank you for suggesting the character names!

Bloggers – I know how much work goes into what you do for free, to support others, to share the word of new releases and books you love. I just want you to know I appreciate you so much!

Special friends – Michelle Dare, T.K. Leigh, MJ Fields, & Gina Whitney, I'd be lost without your friendship!

My beta team – You yell, cry, and threaten me with almost every book—and I love you for it!!! Thank you for your time, your input, and your loyalty. Beth, Dana, Becca, Cheryl, Chelle, Meghan, Kelly, Rachel, Heather, Crystal, Christy, Brittani, & Tabitha—all my love to you after this book!!!

Tabitha – thank you for always standing by my side, helping in any and every way, and giving your honest opinions. I know I can always count on you!

Lisa Hollett, with Silently Correcting Your Grammar – my editor and my friend, thank you for all your help, the last minute penciling me in, the witty messages that always make me laugh, and your honest feedback as a reader and a professional.

ABOUT THE AUTHOR

A.D. Justice is the USA Today bestselling author of the Steele Security Series (Wicked Games, Wicked Ties, Wicked Nights, Wicked Intentions, Wicked Shadows), the Crazy Series (Crazy Maybe, Crazy Baby), the Dominic Powers series (Her Dom, Her Dom's Lesson), the Immortal Obsessions series (Immortal Envy), and a few stand-alone romance novels, such as Completely Captivated, Just One Summer, Envy, and Intent.

When she's not writing, she's spending time with her own alpha male character in their North Georgia mountain home. She is also an avid reader of romance novels, a master at procrastination, a chocolate sommelier, a twister of words, and speaks fluent sarcasm. An avid animal lover, A.D. Justice has two horses, a dog, and two cats.

While the primary focus of her books has been romantic suspense, she has expanded into different sub-genres of romance. Stay tuned to read what she has in store for you!

Connect with her online!
Bookbub: https://www.bookbub.com/authors/a-d-justice
Newsletter: http://www.subscribepage.com/adjustice
Facebook Reader Group:
https://www.facebook.com/groups/angelswickedcrazycrew/

www.authoradjustice.com
adjustice@outlook.com

ALSO BY A. D. JUSTICE

Steele Security Series

Wicked Games

Wicked Ties

Wicked Nights

Wicked Intentions

Wicked Shadows

Dominic Powers Duet

Her Dom

Her Dom's Lesson

The Crazy Duet

Crazy Maybe

Crazy Baby

Stand-alone Novels

Intent

Completely Captivated

Envy (Kindle World novella)

Just One Summer (novella)

Paranormal

Immortal Envy

99877185R00140

Made in the USA
Columbia, SC
16 July 2018

I WANTED TO ASK FOR A DIVORCE.

Instead of the fight I expected, she agreed—with a few stipulations, all of which revolved around our son leaving for college in the fall.

Keeping those promises would be a challenge, no doubt. But all I had to do was uphold my end of the deal then walk away without a backward glance.

Somewhere along the way, our charade became my reality.

With each day that passes, I realize time is once again my enemy. I can't lose her a second time. I'll never walk away—she healed my soul.

SAVING GRACE IS NOW MY ONLY HOPE.

FOR MORE INFORMATION, VISIT
www.authoradjustice.com

ISBN 9781981942312

90000

9 781981 942312